THE
DOMINO
EFFECT

a novel

KRISTIN HELLING

THE DOMINO EFFECT
by Kristin Helling

Printed in the United States of America
First Printing, 2018
ISBN: 978-1-946921-95-6

Adrenaline
An imprint of Wordwraith Books, LLC

705-B SE Melody Lane 149

Lee's Summit, MO 64063
e-mail wordwraiths@gmail.com
website www.wordwraiths.com
Twitter @Wordwraiths

Edited by Ellen Campbell
Cover Design by Austin Helling
Format Design by Kevin G. Summers

Kristin's email author@kristinhelling.com
Kristin's website kristinhelling.com

For Austin
For the Wordwraiths
For the Indiepub group
For Mom and Dad
For Remy

"We're terrible at realizing what goes on in other people's heads because we are trapped inside our own."

—Derren Brown, famous mentalist and illusionist

TABLE OF CONTENTS

ONE

Tanner Copycat

hated this face anyway. He pried his lids open to gaze through the holes in the gauze mask. Through lacerated skin and crushed bone, nobody would know the role he'd played the last few months anyway. With a large amount of money, a plastic surgeon could make him look like whoever he wanted to look like. His days of playing poor, anxiety ridden Tanner were over. Of course, he didn't see the end, beaten in a hospital bed.

Why hasn't he come to see me yet? He complained to himself, thinking of his leader. Any amount of movement brought him pain. But he would be rewarded soon enough. He did everything the man asked of him, and then some. And like clockwork, just as he began to doze off, the door to the hospital room opened.

His first thought was that if it wasn't another nurse checking his vitals, it was more law enforcement. So far and without difficulty, he'd been able to ward off anybody sniffing around with questions by doing what he did best, acting, though he technically wasn't acting, he was in just too much pain to answer any of their questions.

The routine was always the same. They'd come into the room, he'd moan in pain, and the nurses would step in and administer more pain medication. The rest was a blur, but it always made them go away. He wouldn't be able to keep this act up forever, but for now, while he wasn't sure what the next step was, it would do.

But the visitor didn't burst in and approach him, shooting questions and demands. And they didn't come poking around for of his vitals either, like the nurses tended to do every time he was about to get some rest. He almost second guessed the fact that he'd heard the door open at all, and thought perhaps he was hallucinating it, hoping for it, when a shadow loomed over him.

His heart soared with gratitude. "You came," he whispered. He smiled up at the hooded figure, though nobody would be able to tell he was smiling underneath the bandages and gauze. When the man didn't respond, he strained his eyes to see a facial expression. What he could feel of his body tensed, as his understanding of the reason for his visit did a one-eighty in his mind.

And then it hit.

The panic. He was aware all along what this human next to his bed was capable of. It played out in front of him, time and time again.

He followed and played along with his games.

And now, he *was* the game. "I haven't spoken a word to anyone," he choked out the sentence. Hoping the leader would at least let him speak. Hoping he'd listen. Wondering why his room wasn't being monitored at this very moment. This entire time he'd been on lockdown. His room was being watched. How did he get in?

Though the thought did occur to him that perhaps whatever this man had in store for him was better than the fate that awaited him at the end of recovery, once they found out who he really was.

The hooded man reached into his pocket, retrieved something small that fit into the palm of his hand and reached for the IV. He wanted to scream, and shout, and press the call button that was out of his reach.

"I promise I didn't tell them anything. They don't know it's you!" His words came quicker now, he didn't even feel the pain when he moved his mouth. "I did everything you told me to."

Without a word the man injected his IV.

It happened so fast, the cool sensation that rushed through his veins. And he went numb, uncertain if it was because of the vial or fear. As his world grew darker and his lungs began to close, he tried to choke out, "Pro...profess..." though nobody would hear his last words. Nobody except Professor Jensen.

THE DOMINO EFFECT

TWO

Raine Walsh

The aftermath of the most recent events in her life was taking much more of a toll on her than she expected. In her lilac office, the sunlight from the window beaming in, Raine noticed the small specks of dust running through the light and thought about how she was probably breathing that stuff in all the time without realizing it. She sat cross-legged on the floor, the palms of her hands resting on her knees.

Regardless the specks of dust in the air, she breathed deeply, filling her lungs, puffing her chest out, and then releasing. Her chest, lungs, and belly deflated. Again, she breathed in, trying to fill her body with intention and focus, and releasing out anything that was not serving her.

It'd been a while since she had practiced meditation, and that wore on her. The longer away from the craft, the less natural it felt and the more work it became. And the problem with shutting out the rest of the world to try and do the practice, was the fact that she was left with only her own thoughts, which was a far worse scenario.

Her own thoughts always floated back to what had happened. Chloe's boyfriend being murdered in a hit and run. Raine wanted to be there for her sister, as Chloe had been there for her. Though it was almost as if she didn't know how to show support. With the amount of loss she'd dealt with, and the field she worked in, it would seem that it'd be easy for support to come to her, and once again, a natural act. But when it was someone close, somebody who knew her, somebody who shared the same childhood, it was different. Not to mention she had the rest of her feelings to deal with. The fact that she tried to help her client, Tanner, and the mess that that situation had turned out to be.

She put herself in harm's way again. But in her eyes, it was for good reason. Even so, the facts remained the same.

The professor. She had a history of negative interactions with him during her college undergrad. This professor happened to keep popping up everywhere in her field and in her life, many years after she'd just tuned out his existence, and in hindsight, she probably should have turned him in on multiple occasions. But that's not how it had happened. And recently, so many events around her just happened to lead right back to this professor. What were the odds? Too many things lined up for it to be coincidence.

She took it upon herself to show up at his residence, mostly just looking for answers about Alex Wood's death, since Alex had been the professor's student assistant. The two were in contact with each other pretty much every day, and Alex never once mentioned Professor Jensen was going out of town or anything like that. But when she showed up at his house to ask about Alex, the professor was supposedly at his vacation home in Arizona. He supposedly had an alibi there. Well then, it was quite a surprise to everyone who showed up at the professor's mansion the bloodbath that ensued regarding her client, Tanner.

Perhaps that was one reason why she didn't feel closure from this particular nightmare. It was ongoing. She could call or drop by the hospital and see how the Tanner imposter was doing. Of course, nobody had proof that he was actually impersonating Tanner. His face was so badly beaten, that nobody could make out what the guy looked like. And because of Tanner's history with law enforcement and the fact that he was diagnosed with extreme paranoia, it was questionable whether or not his story was the one they believed—especially because he wasn't the one recovering in the hospital.

Her thoughts were interrupted by a knock at the office door. Her head shot up. "Cm'in," she slurred.

The door cracked open and her office partner, ex-boyfriend, and quite possibly the last person on the planet she wanted to see right now peeked in.

"Oh, I'm sorry, is this a bad time? I didn't realize you were meditating."

She looked down at the floor, dropping her hands from her knees to her sides. Before speaking she bit her tongue a moment and tried to think of the most cordial response. The last time they spoke hadn't been so pleasant. Trying to keep from an emotional explosion was a chore. She'd also had some pretty hefty doubts about Marcus's trustworthiness over the last several weeks, and for good reason.

"I was distracted anyway," she responded.

"Can I come in a second?" He remained at the door.

She appreciated that and took it as a form of respect, considering. She nodded and rose from the floor with grace. She leaned against her desk and crossed her arms over her chest, then watched Marcus shut the door and turn to her.

"I just wanted to see how you were doing after all... that happened."

The fact that she couldn't decipher whether he was genuine or not pulled at a part of her psyche that bottled up irritation. She'd known him for so long. They'd been friends, best friends since her early college years. Even after dating him and being on and off all the time, she still couldn't gauge him. Even being an intuitive person.

Am I losing my touch? The thought occurred to her that it could also be her own fault. *Am I holding biases against him that are making me think everything he does has an ulte-rior motive?* She was still mad at him for hiring Lilly behind her back, even though Lilly didn't turn out to be so bad after all. In fact, it was more enjoyable holding a conversation with Lilly than Marcus nowadays.

"I'm fine," she shot back. Short responses. Closed off body language. Wasn't that enough? *He can be so dense sometimes. Doesn't he know when someone's annoyed with him?*

"Are you going to continue working with Heely then, on his cases?" he pressed.

She almost laughed. But his question just proved how out of touch he really was with her.

"What? What's that smirk about?" He sat down on her couch.

She straightened her spine to try and release some of the tension building from him making himself comfortable in her office. "I haven't been working with Heely for quite some time, Marcus." *Surface answers,* she told herself.

"Oh?"

"We're not even on speaking terms actually." She studied his body language.

His ears moved up and then down as he clenched his jaw. He was nervous. *He knows something I don't.*

"He didn't... bug your phone."

Now it was her turn to wear her emotion on her face.   "Well I mean... he did but-"

"Are you and Heely best buds now?" she spat.

Her cheeks were hot. The muscles across her upper back and shoulders tightened. Moments ago she was meditating. She needed to channel that energy again.

Marcus was quiet a moment. "I had him do it."

"Why?"

"I was worried about you. I didn't want anything else bad to happen to you. When you were gone and you weren't answering my calls or texts, and nobody else knew where you were, I turned to the detective. I had him put a tracker in your phone back when I couldn't get a hold of you when you went to his office. It was strictly for safety and I agreed not to access it unless I absolutely had to."

"Why in the hell would you not tell me this? Sounds creepy. Stalker-ish." She began to withdraw inside herself again. She didn't know who this man was right now. Possessive. Anxiety ridden.

"I'm not proud of it. Or how things ended between us, Raine."

She exhaled loudly, loud enough for him to hear.

"You need to research more into the effects that trauma has on the ones that are closest to the victim."

"Sounds a bit self-serving, if you ask me."

"Raine. Just listen."

She was over the conversation. *Why did he come in here again?*

"I think you should take some time off," he finished. "Oh?"
She laughed. "Do you?"

"I'm serious. I think it will be good for you."

"Is that why you asked me about working with Heely?
"Trying to pawn me off?"

"No. I jus—"

"Do you think I'm not capable of handling—"

"Raine!" Marcus cut her off, standing and toweringover
her. "Shut your mouth, for once! Man!"

She pursed her lips and leaned away from him. This
was new, and she didn't like it. She looked at the door, her
only way out. She didn't think he'd hurt her, but she didn't
like his energy one bit. Her eyes quivered. He didn't touch
her, but his energy was powerful and overbearing, and
quite unexpected.

"I'm not asking you to take time off. I'm telling
you. You're not right. You need time. Take a trip. Go on a
vaca-tion. Be there for your sister. Just, something!"

She parted her lips to speak, but his booming voice
continued.

"You'll still get your salary. Lilly can cover your clients, which I've noticed have been quite limited recently
anyway."

He was right. She *had* cut down quite a bit on her clients. But could you blame her? Her experience with treating
clients had not been so great lately. She'd treated Vinnie
and his wife, and didn't even realize that he had been a
serial killer the entire time. She'd treated Tanner before that
whole situation blew up. Who was next? What else would
she miss in sessions, giving humanity the benefit of the
doubt? Why was she always taking on clients that ended up
in dangerous situations? Maybe she just wasn't meant to
be a therapist. Maybe she did need to work on herself
before she could help others. How did she get so far off
path she saw for herself?

She hardly noticed Marcus had gone from the office, leaving her feeling defeated and weak in his wake. No strength to respond. The slam of the door into its frame reverberated a range of emotions through the floor and into her body.

As she looked around the office, at the sitting area, bookshelves, and her desk, she couldn't think of a single thing to take back home with her during her involuntary leave of absence from the clinic. Not a single thing.

Perhaps this was best.

She gathered her bag and made for the door, waving goodbye to Sylvie as though it were any other day, put her head down and marched out the front door, down the stairs.

Walking toward the train, the teeny tiny voice inside her brain began to speak.

Why does Marcus want me far away from the off ce? Far away from him and Lilly? There had to be a reason, other than his deep concern for her psychological well-being.

Perhaps he was working for someone? The person she believed was targeting her since she was taken? Perhaps his concern for her health and well-being wasn't his motive at all.

There was work to do. Her sister still had questions whether or not her boyfriend's killer was connected in any way. The question also remained whether the person who tried to kill Tanner and had been beaten up in the midst of it, *inside* Professor Jensen's house, had acted alone. That, among other mysteries. And now, she didn't have the clinic as a distraction. She had all the time in the world.

THREE

Raine Walsh

Raine unlocked the door to her studio apartment, greeted by her constant in life, a happy-to-see-her Viona swirling around her legs. She patted her head and ears, sat her bag down by the door, then looked up to see the back of her sister's blonde head. The television in front of her was off, and Chloe seemed to be staring off into oblivion. Raine walked into the kitchen and opened a cupboard, pulling out a bottle of wine that she'd been waiting to share. She reached into a drawer and retrieved a corkscrew. Using all her strength, she twisted the metal screw down into the cork and yanked it.

She didn't even bother to grab glasses before she walked with the bottle to the couch. She plopped down next to her bloodshot-eyed sister and held it out to her. Without a word, Chloe took the bottle and tipped it to her lips. She handed it back to Raine, who downed a swig of the sweet red wine, then laid her head on her little sister's shoulder.

They didn't need to speak. Raine sensed how Chloe felt, and the feeling was mutual. Their bond as sisters was enough. Together, they drowned their sorrows.

Tomorrow was a new day, and tomorrow she would no longer engage in her own pity party.

She would rise to action.

But tonight was a different story.

When she woke up, a stream of drool trailed from her lip down to her pillow. She turned in her bed, hitting a big lump. The dog. Surely Viona thought that since she was allowed on the bed while Raine left the apartment—after all it *was* in the family room—that she was entitled to it at nighttime too. Raine didn't mind. Viona kept her warm and offered companionship. The dog gave her the illusion that she was safe.

Raine sat up in her bed. She saw the lump under the crocheted blanket—Chloe passed out. Her own head pulsed. The wine headache.

They'd finished the bottle last night and apparently went back to the kitchen and grabbed another. It wasn't an every night kind of thing, and Raine only had two bottles in her cupboard, or the damage could have been much worse. She mozzied to the kitchen and grabbed some water and aspirin, swallowing the pill and lubricating her dry throat, no doubt from sleeping with her mouth open all night, something out of her control. She held her hand up to her temple as she shifted to the bathroom.

A cold shower ought to wake her up. And then it was go time. She needed to call Josie, the detective in charge of Tanner's case, to see if there was any more information about the man that impersonated and tried to kill Tanner.

She stepped outside a moment. With her hair sopping wet, she leaned against the siding next to her door on the ground floor apartment. She wasn't sure where Josie would be, so she thought she'd try the office first.

"Detective Hatch, please," she asked through the line.

"Hatch." Her voice was unfaltering and strong, tom-boyish and purposeful.

"Hi, Josie, It's Raine Walsh." She heard a shuffle and Josie called over her shoulder, *It's the psychologist!* She wondered exactly what that implied in the office. After all, it *was* Heely's office as well. Surely, they knew more about her than she thought they did. But if she wasn't doing anything questionable, did that matter?

"What can I do for you, Dr. Walsh?"

Raine snapped out of her thoughts again. "I was wanting to check up on my client, Tanner—the guy involved in the copycat case at that Stanford professor's mansion. That... among other things. I have quite a few questions about how everything went down, and with the information you've been able to gather so far, we may be able to help each other."

There was silence on the line a moment before Josie spoke. "Why don't you take a trip down here?" she said.

"Oh?" Raine asked.

"There have been quite a few... developments. It'd be better to speak in person, rather than on an unsecured line."

"All right. I can be in in about an hour."

"I'll see you then." Josie hung up. She was one of those people who didn't close their phone call with a stan-dard *goodbye*. Raine never understood that, how did those kinds of people know that the conversation was over? It was so unsettling and with no closure to the phone call, some-thing that was hard to digest. But that wasn't what bothered Raine about the call. What bothered her was that Josie had information that seemed to be newly developed, and some-thing she didn't want to speak over the phone about. That intrigued Raine to the point of goosebumps down her arms.

They didn't need to know that Raine was on leave from her job. And Marcus didn't need to know that she was working. He wasn't her boss anyway. She went back into the apartment, grabbed more aspirin and water and walked over to the coffee table. She set it down for Chloe to take when she woke. She placed her hand on her sister's back a moment, only the palm of her hand squished into the blanket. There was no movement.

Raine pulled the crocheted blanket back, to see that the lump was a row of pillows from the couch. Chloe was not here.

She must have gotten up early and gone somewhere. *Why would she not leave a note? Does she have the same wine headache that I do?* Then she laughed as she thought perhaps her own wine headache was a symptom of her age. She was in her late twenties, and her drinking and sleeping patterns had definitely changed since she was in college.

It was unusual that her sister would leave and not wake her up, but it was also not unusual that she'd leave on impulse.

Raine scratched Viona, leaned down to her and whispered, "We can go for a run later, okay? I'm in a hurry now." She grabbed her bag and left the apartment, locking it behind her.

There was a lot of misinformation about the professor to refute to law enforcement. The fact that the horrific events took place in his mansion and that he had connections with Alex were in her favor. Maybe Josie had a few more developments about that line of mysteries. Perhaps she would finally get justice for that dirty old man who haunted her throughout her whole career.

Raine closed the door and turned to see Detective Hatch at the window behind her desk. She wasn't sure if she should sit or not, not really knowing where she stood to begin with.

"What's your interest in this case, Dr. Walsh?" Josie asked without turning from the window to look at her, as though she had eyes in the back of her head.

"Uhh..." Raine reached up and ruffled her hair. A nervous tick. She needed to be careful with her answer here, and not make it look like a conflict of interest.

"I'm here in the best interests of my client," she began, speaking about Tanner.

Josie turned from the window and stood behind her desk, offering a hand gesture for Raine to sit in the chair across. Her lips were straight, not cracking a smile. This woman didn't like phone salutations, or real-life greetings. "Yet you weren't at the professor's house to rescue your client, am I correct?"

Wow, she really is a detective. And Raine wasn't expecting to get grilled at this meeting. She looked around to see if there was anyone else near. "No. I had suspicions of the residence and the man who lives there. I thought he was directly involved in another case. Alex Wood, the college student who was killed in a hit and run."

Josie nodded, her eyes glazing over, as though that wasn't the answer she wanted to hear, but it would have to suffice.

"Excuse me, Detective Hatch, but may I ask why you had me come to the station instead of discussing over the phone?" Raine asked.

Josie remained quiet another moment. She finally sat down in the chair behind the desk, though almost at the edge of the chair as though she wasn't allowed to get comfortable.

Raine observed body language clear as day. She was apprehensive. She did not have good news.

Perhaps if she prompted Josie, they could get to the root of her questions sooner. "I know that I don't have any authority in the case concerning my client. But, I'd like to know that the person who did this to him is at least being questioned. Do we even know who that person was to begin with yet? Surely he's had time to recover judging by how much time has passed. I can't imagine how frustrating it must be for Tanner and his family, especially after nobody in law enforcement would believe that he had been stalked to begin with. Nobody believed him that is, until he was dragged into a basement and forced to endure horrific things." She pursed her lips. She read that Josie was letting her speak, as though she was waiting for something to slip. Did she suspect Raine? Surely not. Raine was just being paranoid, considering the circumstances and the lack of information she was given. She gathered that Detective Hatch was also someone who was very perceptive. She was a listener. And an absorber.

"The person taken into custody, the one that your client mauled, his name was Robert Jolie. Does that name ring a bell for you?"

She racked her brain. "No, it does not. Has he been speaking with authorities about what happened?" she asked, almost on the edge of her seat as well. The tension was thick in the room.

"We hadn't gotten the chance."

"What does that mean?"

"Dr. Walsh. Listen to me. You're so quick to jump on my words."

Oh, she's a listener, and *she demands that respect right back.* She closed her lips, forcing herself to bury her annoyance deep down.

"There was a bit of a complication in Jolie's hospital room. He was found dead this morning in his bed. Some reaction with the medication in his IV."

The tiny hairs on Raine's arms stood straight up. A lump caught in her throat. "What? How—Was the room not being monitored?"

"The nurses did a routine check not long before, and of course they had his room guarded, since he was a suspect."

Raine couldn't believe her ears. This man, Robert, was supposed to be the key to catching Professor Jensen. He must have had information, considering the crime scene was inside the basement of the professor's mansion, and the professor was apparently not home—this being someone who was hired to watch his residence while he was gone. Dead men can't speak. Dead men can't convict a man who deserved it. "Are you sure..." She tried to swallow and heard the gulp in the quiet room. "—that nobody went into that room that wasn't supposed to be there? I just... I'm not sure I buy it."

Josie closed her eyes and nodded. "I agree. It smells funny to me. Foul play. Our number one suspect is now dead. It's a bit too easy if you ask me."

Even though she was stern and somewhat hard to pin down, Raine was beginning to like this detective. She didn't take everything for what it appeared to be. Raine hoped she'd be thorough—exactly what Raine needed.

"And what about questioning the next best suspect in the case?" she asked.

"Who do you think that is?" Josie asked.

"Dr. Dill Jensen of course. The owner of the residence."

Josie opened her mouth but Raine interrupted again. "I know that he was out of town when the incident happened, and that he had a decent alibi—" She tried to refrain from rolling her eyes. "But there has to be something there."

"Jensen was cleared."

Raine tensed once more. *Of course he was!* "And what of the crime scene?"

"It was closed out."

It took everything not to leap up from the seat and scream. *What were they thinking? How could he get off so easy?* "Well now what? What stands of Tanner's case?" she asked. "Where is his peace of mind?" She was trying to keep her voice from shaking.

"His peace of mind is that the man who tried to kill him is dead."

Raine closed her mouth, grabbed for her bag, and stood up. "Thank you, for your time, Detective Hatch. There's not much else to say here."

"Well, I appreciate your interest in helping us with this case. I wish you luck with your client, and hope you're able to help him cope with what he went through."

Little did she know that Raine had transferred all of her clients. She couldn't help Tanner anymore.

And it felt as though she couldn't help anyone. The words Josie said, *his peace of mind is that the one who tried to kill him is dead*, did not sit well with her. Because she knew, even if nobody else believed her, that the man that tried to kill him, was in fact, not dead.

FOUR

Raine Walsh

As she walked from the train to her apartment, she thought about Chloe's absence this morning. It was weird. Her sister had been staying with her since the incident, and they always communicated with each other when they were coming in and out. She turned into the courtyard of her apartment, and noticed immediately that her front door stood ajar, just a crack. Her intuition boosted a queasy feeling in her stomach. Something wasn't right.

She pushed the door open and was not greeted by her four-legged baby. Chloe was nowhere in sight. Did she come back and take Viona for a walk? Could the pup not wait until Raine was back and guilted Chloe into it?

And then Raine saw it. Viona's leash hanging by the door. The dog never left the apartment without it. If Chloe was to take her somewhere, she'd have that leash. She turned around, nearly tripping on herself and shouted out the front door.

"Viona!" Her heart sped up, the adrenaline making each of her limbs shake involuntarily. She had no idea when this happened. Of course, the door stuck sometimes, and even if it was locked from the inside and then pulled shut, if you didn't wait for the click, it sometimes popped back open. Perhaps Chloe did this earlier and wasn't thinking that the door could pop back open.

She pulled her phone out and dialed her sister's number, her finger shaking over the small number keys.

It rang and rang, then went to voicemail.

"Shit!" She tossed her phone onto the counter, grabbed Viona's leash and ran out of the

apartment. She rounded the corner of the building onto the main road, which was busy. "Vi! Viona!" she shouted. *I leave her in the care of my sister, thinking she's responsible enough to watch her but she loses my dog!* In those few short moments, she thought of all the possibilities, including never being able to find her dog again.

Someone could have pulled up in a car and snatched the beautiful, social, pit mix, forcing her into a fighting ring.

Viona could have gotten hit by a car on one of these busy roads.

The dog could have wandered and wandered to exhaustion, excited to explore at first and catch all the smells, and then never be able to find her way home.

Raine felt her heart breaking, her eyes welled with tears as she shouted Viona's name. She had no idea who was on the street, what cars were there, or what other people were present. She only cared about finding her pup and bringing her home. As she passed a deep, dark alley between buildings, she thought she caught a glimpse of something. Movement by the dumpster. Was it a homeless person? A raccoon?

"Viona?" she shouted down the alley, her voice echoing off the brick wall at the back. Chains rattled. The rabies license and the one with her Viona's name and Raine's number etched onto it, clanging together as the pup perked her head up.

Raine dropped to her knees. "Vi! Come here girl!" Was she hallucinating through her blurry eyes? Her dog came running toward her now. The tan dog drenched up to her belly with mud. "How long have you been out here, girl? Where's Auntie Chloe?" Raine quickly maneuvered the leash onto Viona's collar and stood up with whatever strength she had left, relieved but still shaking from the adrenaline.

She hadn't gotten far, but it still looked like she'd been out here for quite a while. Raine rushed back home, not even sure if *she* had closed the door in the frantic sprint out of it. As she rounded the corner, she saw that she had. She went inside with the dog, slamming the door shut behind her. "You need a bath!" she told Viona, walking her on the leash straight to the bathroom. "I guess we won't be taking that run today, girl." She put her in the bathroom and unhooked the leash, to contain the mud. "You stay here, I'll be right back." She slipped back out of the bathroom and ran to her phone.

With her fingers still wobbly, she pulled up Chloe's number again and texted her. "Found Viona. Where the hell are you?" She sent the text, and then immediately regretted it. What if Chloe didn't even realize the door had popped back open? She didn't want to be mean to her but the fact of the matter was that she could have lost the thing in Raine's life that she loved the most because of a careless mistake. The whole thing made her feel immensely guilty.

After she sent the text and turned to go back to the bathroom to wash Viona, she heard a vibration sound. She looked down at the counter. It wasn't her phone. "What the hell..." She walked closer to the bathroom and stood a moment, listening to the quiet sound of her studio apartment, the usual fan noise from the vents, and a small moan from Viona not liking the fact that she was cooped up in the bathroom. The vibration noise happened again. She heard it coming from the television area. She walked toward the couch, and then she saw it.

Chloe's phone. Sitting on the coffee table. Vibrating from receiving Raine's text.

She froze.

Chloe would never leave without her phone.

Something was wrong.

Raine grabbed her sister's phone and with her own phone in the other hand, she dialed the next person she could think of, and leaned forward at the end of the couch. With each ring, her stomach knotted even more. On the third ring, he picked up.

"Hey, how's it going?"

"Arie," she said.

"What's wrong?" he asked.

"Something happened to Chloe. Chloe's gone."

"What? Where are you?"

"I'm at home, and when I got here the door was open and Viona was gone and I had to find her."

"Whoa, slow down, babe. Deep breaths, okay? It's going to be okay. What do you mean Viona was gone?"

She heard him shuffling on the other line. "Well when I got home today, the door to my apartment was open. Viona was gone but her leash was here so I knew she got out—"

"Your door sticks. Was Chloe aware of that? Maybe she just left in a hurry and didn't realize?"

"I thought that too, but when I came back I found her cell on the coffee table. She would never leave without her phone. I don't know what to do. I'm freaking out!"

"Deep breaths. I'm already in the car, okay? I'm coming. Just... lock your door. You said you found Vi?"

"Yes, she was down the street a little, in an alley. She was soaked."

"Okay... Uhh stay with her, I'm coming. Okay?"

Raine heaved a sigh. She felt comforted knowing that he was on his way, but also terrified by what could have happened. What could he do to help her besides be support? "What if something bad happened, Arie?" She began to choke up, her voice rising.

"Just keep doing breathing exercises. Don't let your mind wander, okay? You always think of all the worst possibilities. We can put our minds together and figure something out. Chloe has been distressed about Alex's passing. Maybe this was a fluke. She was feeling bad and split, not thinking about anything else. It could be as easy as that. Don't immediately think the worst."

"Arie..." she said his name matter-of-factly, as though she knew better than to take his comforting words and fully believe them.

"I know. I know a lot of bad things have happened to you. But that doesn't mean that the streak continues. Just stay positive and keep all the options open. I'm on my way."

They hung up. She sat a moment on the couch, her head in her hands as she allowed the phone to drop to the ground. She looked up at Chloe's phone again.

It wasn't right that she'd leave it.

Was it possible Chloe was going through some phase where she thought everyone was so reliant on their phones and she was going to go a day without it? If that were the case, she would have left a note. No. Something was entirely wrong.

Viona let out another moaning whine. She'd forgotten she left her dog in the bathroom. She got up and grabbed a few towels on the way.

She dropped the towels by the door just as a thought entered her mind. "One minute, Vi." She called out to the bathroom door, and then crossed over into the kitchen. She locked the door. If they came for Chloe, whoever *they* were, they could very well come back for her.

Then she looked around the apartment. *I need something heavy...* There were a lot of potentials, she just needed to decide what she'd be able to move. There was a cabinet pressed up against the wall between the bathroom and front door. Something she'd stick mail or her keys on. It was a cabinet she'd had since she first moved to San Francisco. She'd picked it up at a flea market when she was looking to furnish her apartment, back in the days when everything seemed easier.

Today, the cabinet would provide her security, no matter false or not, and the reassurance of barricading the only way in and out of the apartment. She heaved into the side of it with her shoulder and all the strength she had in her small frame, letting a grunt escape her lips.

The cabinet dresser budged. She used the momentum from that push to heave into it again, sliding the heavy wood across the vinyl flooring. She continued to shove it until she heard the *thunk* against the door. Out of breath, she leaned back and admired her work. It might have been silly, but she needed it. She went into the kitchen, grabbed some peanut butter dog biscuits she'd baked the other day.

She grabbed both hers and Chloe's phones and opened the door to the bathroom. Viona tried to push out. "You are *not* getting mud all over this apartment." She kicked the towels into the bathroom, and shut the door behind her. The tiny hairs on the back of her neck stood up as she placed Chloe's phone on the back of the toilet seat.

She sent a quick text to Arie that told him to call her when he got there, because she'd barricaded the door, and then she bent down to Viona. The dog licked her cheek with her sandpaper tongue.

Raine grabbed the dog's face. "What did you see, girl? What happened today, hmm?"

The pup wagged her tail, backed up and smelled the air. Raine tossed her one of the peanut butter treats and then turned the water on. She wished she could read Viona's mind. The dog experienced what happened to Chloe, and who took her, if that was the case. In any normal scenario, one would call the police. But she hadn't been missing more than twenty-four hours, and Raine had pretty much burned her bridges with Heely. She wasn't buddy-buddy with Detective Hatch either. She truly felt like there was nobody out there that would help, or even listen to her. It would be a complete waste of time.

She coaxed Viona into the tub, however gracefully a pit mix could be coaxed, and used a plastic cup to splash the dog with water. Viona didn't seem to mind the water. It was calming to wash Viona, the mud and stink swirling down the drain, and she didn't even want to think about what the grunge contained. Though she found it peaceful, everything presently going on played over and over in her head.

She suspected the person was not somebody after Chloe. This person was after Raine. And the guilt weighed her down, that she'd involved her sister in anything that was going on. Her life was a big mess, and her sister was now subjected to that.

Before, it was easy to keep the ones she loved at a distance, both literally and figuratively. Her family always saw her as independent rather than standoffish. And after a year or two, she just stopped going home for family holidays and events, claiming that she was busy and couldn't get away. Having Chloe here was such a different dynamic. And she failed her sister.

She hoped Chloe was okay, wherever she was.

Viona hopped out of the tub before Raine was ready for her and shook, water flying in every direction. She soaked Rainc, leaving her smelling like a wet dog herself.

She threw a towel over Viona's body and rubbed it into her fur until the towel was damp. It would take a few to dry her. Before she was finished, her phone beeped. Raine jumped with surprise and lunged forward, scaring Viona, who leaped back, banging into the tub.

Raine lit up her phone to the message from Arie that read, "Here". She sighed, getting up from her knees. For a split second she'd thought it was her sister. She opened the door and Viona charged out of the bathroom, running all over the studio apartment with her clean fur, jumping from the sofa to the bed.

She began to pull the cabinet back, just enough to get to the door. "Arie?" she called and placed both hands on the wood.

"I'm here."

She unlocked it and swung it open, flinging herself into his arms.

His arms wrapped around her. "You smell like you've been at *my* work all day," he said, referring to the dog shelter.

"Vi... she was soaking and stinky when I found her. I gave her a bath." Raine was out of breath and trying to find the words she needed to communicate with Arie.

"Let's get inside. okay?"

She backed into her apartment with him in tow. She turned to lock the door behind them as he eyeballed the cabinet.

"You moved that by yourself?" he asked. "It took two of us to get it in here when you moved in."

She nodded. She was drained. Hungry. Exhausted, both mentally and physically. It hadn't been long since she got home, and her muscles were already aching from the dog bath and moving the cabinet. But none of that mattered. None of it. Because it was dark outside now, and her sister was still gone.

Now that Arie was here, it was time to put their heads together and figure out what happened, then do something about it. She wasn't sure how much time she had.

She followed Arie to the couch and sat down next to him.

He rested his hand on her knee. She looked up at his face, realizing that he hadn't even noticed he'd naturally placed it there.

"Have you thought of any possibilities of where she could be?" he asked. "Is there still a chance that maybe she went on her own volition, and just wasn't thinking about her phone or telling you?" The shakiness in his voice told her he thought it was a long shot.

She shook her head. "It's not like her."

"Maybe she's upset about Alex."

"Of course she is but it doesn't seem right. None of this. I didn't even get a chance to tell her that the person they had in custody who hurt my client was killed in the hospital."

"Wait, what?"

She watched him lurch back in surprise, the emotions apparent on his face. The crease as his eyes showed confusion, a piece of his ashen hair falling on his forehead. "How in the world do you know he was killed?" he asked.

"This all leads back to the same person. All of it. This person was the prime suspect in a case that took place at the mansion of Jensen."

"*The* Professor Jensen?"

"Yes. And now the prime suspect is dead. Which means he can't talk, right? And not only that, but I asked the detective if they'd been questioning the professor, and she said he'd been cleared of all charges. It's him, Arie. And he probably has Chloe too."

"Is he capable of... You know?"

She sat a moment. "I'd like to think not. But my thoughts are racing right now."

"You think he's at his house?"

"Chances are slim, especially if police are still poking around there."

Arie nodded. "Where do we even start then?"

"I have a crazy idea." She used the word she hated using. *Crazy.* But she couldn't find any other word to fit this idea. It was more farfetched than anything she'd thought in a while. And if she was wrong about this, then it could take her far away from the real problem, making the outcome much, much worse.

"All right. Let's hear it then." Viona was pushing herself into Arie at his feet. She was always happy to see him.

"When this entire incident happened, they said he wasn't home. He was at a vacation home in Arizona."

"Oh. Raine."

"Said he had a pretty solid alibi."

"Arizona is so far away."

"It's my sister, Arie. And I know he has her. He's been trying to get to me for years. I always turn him down. Well he has my attention now."

"I can go with you. It's dangerous. You, going after her alone. If he really does have her—"

She shook her head, backing up on the couch, her eyes welling up with emotion.

"Come on. Look at everything we've been through together."

"I don't want you hurt too. I've already dragged my sister into this."

"I don't want *you* hurt."

"I can take care of myself."

"I didn't say you couldn't. But I could be your back-up. What if—" he stifled a small laugh, "I followed behind you but didn't tell you. That way you have the illusion that you're alone, but at the right time I could step in and help you."

Her lips twitched up into the small hint of a smile. "You're stubborn."

He laughed. "Not nearly as stubborn as you. How do you know the address?" he asked.

"Chloe told me that she took Alex's notebook from his stuff. I think he wrote it in there when he was in charge of assignments while the professor was gone."

"Wow, that's lucky... and smart that she snatched it. Considering..."

Raine nodded. Now that Alex was gone and she saw the wear and tear it caused on her sister firsthand, she felt guilty for not giving him a solid chance. She'd hated him from the get go because of his connection with the professor, something he didn't even know the repercussions of. He was just trying to have an 'in' in the psychology department. He had no idea what he was getting himself into. And of all the boys at that university, her sister found him? But that was beside the point.

"But if it's not in his notebook… I know who I need to speak to, to get it," she said softly. She stood from the couch and shuffled around the room, throwing on a hoodie and trying to rack her brain for anything else she might need. "And I have to hurry, before it's too late."

"Who?" Arie asked, rising to his feet as well.

Viona paced the room, following behind Raine, clearly feeling her energy.

"I need to go back to my office. Lilly will know."

"Do you trust her? I thought you hated her!"

Raine looked up at him. "She's not so bad. I just need to make sure that I can do it without Marcus seeing me. I don't trust him and I don't want him knowing where I am. You know that tracker in my phone?"

Arie perked up.

"Marcus. It wasn't Heely like I thought. Well it was... only he was doing it for Marcus." She sighed. She left out the tidbit that she also didn't want Marcus to see her because she wasn't supposed to be going in to the office.

"I'm ready."

"What about Vi?" he asked.

Raine looked down at her pup and her eyes reflected the sadness she felt in her heart when she thought about it. She wished she could take her. She knelt down and rubbed behind Vi's ears.

"It's okay, Raine. I'll take care of her."

Raine's eyes welled up with tears, blurring her vision. "You have no idea how much you saying that means to me," she whispered. She walked over to Arie and placed her hand behind his head, leaned in and kissed him. Salty tears moistened their lips as she closed her eyes in the kiss. She leaned back. "Thank you, Arie. I'll keep in contact with you, okay?" she said, reassuring him while she looked him in the eyes.

"I sure hope you're right about all of this," he whispered back.

"Me too," she responded, her confidence faltering.

FIVE

Detective Heely

J onah Heely was free from jail, and free from the insti-
tution of the police force. From some stroke of luck, or
nepotism, he had the ability to finish the work he started
on his own. A reborn detective. Private eye. Of course, he
wouldn't be able to reap the benefits of the resources of the
police, unless he kept in contact with some of his friends on
the police force, but perhaps he didn't need their resources.
Perhaps he had all the tools he needed to solve this mystery.

It was the mystery that he felt wasn't a mystery at all.
He just needed to prove it. It all started when he was assigned a case where a woman was found unconscious in a
landfill by some blue collar workers. The story just got cra-
zier from there. He thought he was in good with her, and she
even helped him to solve a few cases, however, that's where
it ended. This girl either had the worst luck in the world and
was a magnet for danger—or she was the cause of it, in some
master plan that followed every case he'd come in contact
with. He guessed the latter.

There was no way in hell that she wasn't a part of each
of those cases in some way or another, and he was going to
prove it. She was going to slip. Mess up. And he was going

to be there to catch it. Solve the case that had consumed so much of his life. He was going to actually prove to his father what a great detective he was and how smart he was for solving the case of this mastermind murderer once and for all.

As he left his father's office, he crossed the street to his favorite taco shack. His stomach had grumbled, and once he realized it wasn't grumbling from nerves, but from the fact that he hadn't fed himself in more than half a day, he knew he had to stop someplace before heading back home to his new office. Though working from home for him wasn't a new development because he'd been using it as his office the entire time he was on his suspension. And he wanted to get back there as fast as he could, since getting the green light to continue his work. He could not let his father down, after he'd helped him dodge jail time. He could not let himself down. Too much was at stake for him not to solve this series of cases.

Jonah stood behind a couple at the window of the taco shack. He didn't need to look at the menu. It was a given he'd be getting two barbacoa soft tacos with the hot sauce. He reached up and tossed his hair a minute, forgetting how stupid it looked slicked over to the side, the way he always wore it when he went to see his parents.

He ordered his tacos, laughing that the cashier knew his name. They were a family owned establishment, and he visited frequently enough to be considered a regular. After he paid, he backed up to a tree, leaned against it, and crossed his arms over his chest. He watched as other people waiting for their food cricked their necks down to look at their phones. Full families, not even paying attention to each other. Couples together, yet not together because they were connected with their digital worlds. He also realized how dangerous it was for people to do this. Unaware of their surroundings. Vulnerable to creeps that could be watching them from afar. *Creeps like him?* Naw, he was watching for research and observation. He spent most of his time people watching.

A man that walked up to the taco shack caught his eye. Mainly because he was rather attractive, with his dark hair and smooth tanned skin. His hair was clean cut around his ears and neck, his shirt a plunging v neck. He turned to the other person with him, another guy.

Jonah's heart caught in his chest. But not in a good way. In a pinching, throbbing, sinking way.

It was Benjamin. His ex-boyfriend. Benjamin was with this hot guy. Go figure.

Why would he come to MY taco shack!? He knows this is my shack!

The attractive guy turned his head in Jonah's direction.

Without being completely obvious, Jonah slid all the way around to the other side. He pushed his back up against the trunk, his spine straight, and ignored the hard, rough bark that cut into his shirt. His chest rose and fell.

Please don't see me, he pleaded.

He allowed several minutes to pass, and then peeked around the trunk. They were still there, he presumed waiting for their food. He saw his own tacos sitting on the pickup counter. He sighed. The employees probably thought he'd left, which wouldn't be completely out of the ordinary. They knew he had to leave in a hurry sometimes. He hoped they left his food on the counter for a little longer. Long enough for Ben to leave so he could go pick it up and not have to face an awkward conversation.

After glancing at his glorious tacos which he no longer had an appetite for, he looked at Benjamin with the hottie and wondered how long they'd been together. He wouldn't have judged them right off the bat if Benjamin wasn't so handsy with the guy. Placing his hand on the guy's lower back. Throwing his head back and laughing with his perfect-ly white teeth. Probably at something that wasn't even that funny. What he first thought was a spark of jealousy in his gut he quickly realized was loneliness.

He tore his eyes away from them and placed his back against the far side of the tree again. Since he had been suspended from his job and got lost in researching, he'd lost his relationship. Of course, he and Benjamin were on the rocks to begin with, and his obsession and lack of showering was just the final straw for his partner. At one time they were happy. They'd had a stable, solid relationship for quite some time before Ben got bored, or so he could only assume.

Jonah was such a homebody, and Benjamin always had a problem with the fact that Jonah was more reserved and guarded about his sexuality in public. He didn't want to be a stereotypical gay man, whatever that meant.

He also didn't want to be alone forever. He was used to coming home from work to a meal on the table, or perhaps preparing the meal together, or going out to eat. He enjoyed the Friday night Netflix menu surfing, trying to decide on what to watch and end up not watching anything but the menu. All of those things were gone from his life, and he had no desire to seek them right now. They were a distraction, and he was busy.

But that part of him deep inside was vacant right now and watching his ex brought it to the surface.

Maybe he should get a dog?

Better yet, the void could be temporarily filled with his first love. *The work.* And it was. His work as a detective was more fulfilling than any other companion could bring him. It was enough. It made him whole.

Perhaps he should just march out there and get his food, pretending like he didn't see the boys to begin with. To test and see if Benjamin would acknowledge him, or if he'd also dodge him. That'd be interesting. Perhaps Jonah could act like everything was great.

After all, he *did* clean up before going to visit his father. Last time he'd seen Benjamin, that wasn't the case. Perhaps Benjamin would get the idea that Jonah had moved on and was living a better life. What was so bad about an ex thinking that? Perhaps it'd be an ego boost for himself, if nothing else.

Without another thought, he burst out from behind the tree, looking back and forth to see if anybody had noticed him. Like before, everyone was preoccupied doing whatever it was they were doing, and it seemed as though nobody even cared.

Eye on the prize. The taco prize.

He reached the taco shack, the employees hustling busily in the back as he snatched up his food and placed a five dollar bill in its place for a tip.

"Aye, Jonah, 'ave a good one!" The older man shouted after him, and Heely raised his hand to wave goodbye. He headed back to his car at a brisk walk, hopped inside and laid the box of tacos down on the passenger seat.

He never did see Benjamin and hottie as he picked up the food and walked back to his car.

Perhaps he'd hallucinated them? No, the thought of hallucinating them was a pipe dream. They were there. Plain as day. And he dodged them like a coward.

It was the last time he'd do that.

Jonah slammed the door to his apartment shut and set the tacos down on the counter. He flipped open the Styrofoam lid and stuffed one of the barbacoa tacos into his mouth. Lettuce and cheese fell out the back end. After a few more bites standing at the kitchen counter, he walked into the sitting area and stared up at his wall brain map.

He realized how crazy and elaborate it looked, and he'd be embarrassed to have anybody over. But it'd been a while since he'd had anyone stay with him, or visit for that matter. And his encounter at the taco shack just reinforced how important it was that he solved this case.

He followed the red strings pinned over the map, making the connection between each one.

Each perpetrator.

Each outcome.

It started with his first. The prison case. There was information up on this board that law enforcement had probably never seen. Jonah researched and dug into the people involved in this case.

The Warden. Allen Voyer. He was a real-estate mogul. Rich. Owned the skyscraper where he turned the penthouse into a prison. Even though when police got there, it was torn apart. He, himself did not see it set up. But he gathered details from the times he'd spoken with Brandon Perez, Megan, Arie, and even Raine. Though evidence wasn't there, all of their stories matched up. Still so many pieces unsolved.

This guy. The Warden. Supposedly murdered by Megan, he'd graduated from Stanford University. Back when he was in college, he'd interviewed for the infamous experiment the department of psychology put on. The Stanford Prison Experiment. He wasn't accepted.

How was Raine Walsh connected to this man, besides her abduction? She'd also graduated from Stanford. Although a small connection, it was still a tie, and he needed to concentrate and focus on all ties.

Moving on.

The next case. The series of murders that happened in plain sight, using the bystander effect to the perpetrators advantage. The killer: Vinnie Wilson. Now this guy— this guy was hard to pin down. And he'd played a little game of cat and mouse with Heely on several occasions before he was caught. This guy was a loser who worked at the DMV. He was an unlikely villain in an average situation. He had a wife and a small baby, which was unusual for his criminal profile.

It was Jonah's fault that Raine was involved in this one. Had he not gone to her office and asked for her help and expertise in the case, would she have been involved at all? He stared at his board, following once again, the red string from Raine to Vinnie. A new string. Not the one that tied her to Vinnie, through himself.

Vinnie Wilson was one of Raine's clients. She was his therapist. She was very cryptic and secretive when it came to questioning her about the time with him in her office. Said: *patient confidentiality*. But it was important to the case. Why would she not share the information that she'd discovered in those sessions? Did she have insight that the police force didn't?

He could have gotten a warrant. But it didn't matter. Because soon enough, Vinnie was caught with a knife in his back. Literally stabbed in the back by his wife. *Some marriage*.

But there was another string coming from Vinnie as well. It didn't lead directly to Raine, but to another square that Raine branched off of. The same square that led to Allen Voyer. That was Stanford University.

Vinnie Wilson had also been a student there. Not at the same time as Allen, and not at the same time as Raine. But a student nonetheless. Raine *had* to know that from her sessions. Somehow, Vinnie knew Raine attended Stanford. She had her degree framed in her office. It was public domain.

Moving on to the most recent case.

Jonah followed the board to the section he'd been working on. The section he added to during his suspension. Should he have had a home visit by any of the counselors or even his father, perhaps he wouldn't have been cleared.

But nobody came. And he was let off. And he could continue his work.

The newest section was about Alex Wood.

And Raine's client, Tanner.

Her connection to both of these people was uncanny.

Alex was Raine's sister's boyfriend. Through Marcus, Jonah also found out that Raine hated Alex. He was an assistant to a very prestigious professor of psychology at the university. The same professor who owned the house where Tanner was found. The same house that *Raine* led the police to. The strings were all over the place here, pinned into the photo of Raine multiple times.

In the case of Tanner in the basement, he had much less information. Detective Josie Hatch was on the front lines on that case. And when he tried to reach out to her, she refused to give him any information, and told him to go take a vacation. That was frustrating. Of course, she was being professional, but she was blocking him from information he needed.

He couldn't find out all the information he wanted about Alex Wood and Tanner. Alex, a student of Stanford, just like the others.

But the case didn't end there. Jonah had overheard someone talking about the fact that there was some weird experiment conducted in that basement.

And that was very interesting. Very interesting indeed.

Jonah stared at the board, forgetting the fact that he had food on the counter behind him. It wasn't important anymore. He followed the lines from photo to photo until it hit him. It wasn't a person making the connection here.

It was a location. Setting. A character of its own. It was the start of all these killers.

It was the school. The university.

That was it! That was the link. He ran into the kitchen and pulled open his junk drawer, rustling through the batteries and keys and pens and everything else that made its way in there. He pulled out a fat, red, permanent marker. Then he rushed back over to the wall, nearly slamming his hip into the corner of the island in his kitchen. He reached up and circled the photo of Stanford, over and over and over again.

Each case had something to do with some sort of psychological experiment. It was what attracted him to Raine to begin with. The fact that she had an education and creden-tials in psychology.

First, The Stanford Prison Experiment.

Second, the origin of the term 'the bystander effect', marked by that first victim discovered in the lobby of the apartment building. The eerie connection to the Kitty Genovese case that took place in the sixties.

Third, well... he wasn't quite sure what the third case was because he couldn't get his hands on it— blocked by Detective Hatch.

If he hadn't cut Raine out, he might have been able to get some more information about it. He knew, because he saw her at the police station with Detective Hatch, without a doubt she was at the scene of the crime when everything came to a head, per usual. Perhaps he should rekindle his relationship with her. Keep her close. She hadn't seemed to suspect he was on to her.

Marcus could have messed that up with his dumb tracker. He was so lucky he wasn't charged for that. Stupid move. Well, smart move so that he could keep tabs on her, stupid move because she found it.

She wasn't so dumb, that girl.

So that was it. He needed to take a drive to the univer-sity and poke around a little bit. He needed to go to the place that started it all for Raine Walsh.

SIX

Raine Walsh

She couldn't remember the drive from her apartment to her office. It was nearing the end of the work day there. Once again, Arie allowed her to take his car. She was grateful for his presence in her life lately. He was so... selfless. And he was always there for her at the drop of a hat. She couldn't help but wonder what she ever did to deserve him in her life. His caring was unlike any other she'd experienced.

Raine needed to remember to show him how much she appreciated him when she returned. Yes, that was positive thinking. *When* she returned. Not if. That was the mindset she needed to have right now.

She parked across the street from her office, not in the lot they parked in for work, but in front of the building to monitor whether or not Marcus would leave first. She looked down at the passenger seat at the two phones: Hers and Chloe's. She'd decided to bring it just in case. She picked up Chloe's. The office wouldn't recognize that number. She dialed.

"Thank you for calling the offices of Drs. Altor, Walsh, and Everstein, how may I help you?"

"Hey, Sylvie, it's Raine."

"Oh hi, how are you?"

"I'm okay, I don't have much time. Just, pretend like you're speaking with a potential client if Marcus is nearby, okay?" She hoped Sylvie would be loyal.

"Uh, we do have a nine o'clock opening next Wednesday if that would work?"

She heard typing in the background and couldn't help but smile. "Thank you. I just need you to do something for me, please. Go tell Lilly to let Marcus leave first. I need to have a conversation with her... alone. And it's urgent. But I can't let Marcus know about it. Please."

"All right, I'd love to help you with that! I've got you booked, okay?"

She felt that Sylvie's voice shook toward the end of the sentence. She could count on Sylvie, but it was asking a lot to ask her to lie. "Thank you so much. I owe you one."

She ended the call and slumped down in the seat. Now all she had to do was wait. Which was the last thing she wanted to do right now. But she couldn't just aimlessly drive toward another state without a destination.

Her peripheral vision caught a black car coming from the driveway that led to the parking lot in the back of the building. *Marcus.* She ducked down even farther.

He wouldn't recognize the car she was in. It was Arie's. Or Arie's neighbor's to be exact. The neighbor had a sharing agreement with him. And Marcus had never seen Arie driving it. He wouldn't suspect Raine was there.

Why didn't she want Marcus knowing she was there? First off, because he basically suspended her in a passive-aggressive way. He would not be happy if he saw her stalking the office when he'd told her to go on a vacation away from the place. And secondly, she didn't trust him. She didn't want him knowing anything about her whereabouts. She wasn't entirely sure he didn't have something to do with what had been going on, with the little clues here and there.

The thought often crossed her mind that she might be extremely paranoid, which would be understandable, but better safe than sorry.

She preferred to be safe, period. Something she hadn't had the luxury of in quite a long time.

As soon as Marcus's car turned down the road and out of sight, she exhaled, not realizing that she'd been holding her breath.

"Come ooon," she pleaded, looking back up the driveway. If Marcus was gone, what was the hold-up for Lilly? The moment she thought it, she saw a figure walking up the driveway. It was her.

Her legs looked restricted in her tight pencil skirt as she booked it down the driveway toward the car. Only she didn't come to the car, she stopped at the curb and looked up and down the street, conspicuous, but confused.

Raine rustled to roll the window down. "Here!" she yelled, a little less than discreet.

Lilly's head turned and then she walked toward the car, rounding it to the passenger's side.

Raine unlocked it, as she pulled the door handle and tucked inside.

Her eyes were wide orbs behind her cat eyed glasses. "What the hell is going on here?" she asked.

"Thank you so much for listening to Sylvie. You didn't tell Marcus, did you?" she asked.

"No." She crossed her arms over her chest. "You want to tell me what's going on?"

"I need your help."

"I can see that."

Raine was starting to like Lilly, but it was comments like that that set her back again. She was loaded with sarcastic, pretentious one-liners. "I need you to give me the address of Professor Jensen's vacation home." She spat it out without any context.

Lilly was quiet a moment, as though she were trying to absorb what Raine just laid on the table. "What makes you think I'd have that?"

Raine's thoughts were running at a million miles a minute—she didn't have time to think about her words before they escaped her lips and she didn't have the time to spend explaining things either. "You're a colleague. I know he's invited colleagues for retreats there. I know he's probably talked about it at some time, compared neighborhoods with other professors in the teacher's lounge. He had to have talked about it sometime!" Her voice was nearing desperation.

"Raine. What is going on? Why are you coming here in secret? Acting frantic and anxiety ridden. Your body language is screaming at me right now. Why are you asking for your old professor's residence? And why do you... smell like wet dog?" She crunched up her face and backed her head up to the window.

"I don't have time to explain right now." Raine slumped back, closing her eyes. She was sinking.

"Does this have anything to do with Jensen being let off that case that involved your client?" Lilly asked.

"How do you know about that?" she asked, trying to read the expressions on Lilly's face, which were quite non-expressive. She was good at that.

"Because the university professors talk."

"See!"

"I have the address, Raine," she said quietly.

"What gives?"

"I just want to make sure you aren't going to do anything stupid!"

Raine heaved a huge sigh. "I think he's kidnapped my sister, okay!" There. She said it. Now how would that be received? Should she have trusted Lilly with this information to begin with?

"What? Why in the hell would you think that?"

"I told you I didn't have time to explain. Now are you going to help me or not?"

"Why don't you go to the police?"

"He's escaped the police! And I'm not exactly on good terms with them anyway right now. That's a long story."

Lilly looked down into her lap. "Hang out here a moment," she said quietly, opening the door.

Raine leaned forward and grabbed her wrist. Lilly looked at her.

"Can I trust you?" she asked with every ounce of genuine truth in her eyes.

She tipped her chin in a solid nod.

Raine believed her. She let go of her wrist and watched Lilly march back into the office. The moments she sat in the silent car were grueling. Would Lilly betray her? Would she even come back at all? The silence quickly became a ringing in her ears, and time became irrelevant.

It wasn't long before Lilly came trotting back down the driveway. She looked back and forth as she crossed the road and walked to the car.

Raine rolled the driver's side window down.

Lilly handed her a post-it note with an address scrawled on it. "It took me a minute to search my email, but this is it."

Raine took the paper, grazing Lilly's hand as she secured it. "Thank you," she whispered.

"Please tell me you have some sort of backup for this?"

Raine smiled. "I do. And thank you for caring about me. Like I said before, I'd really appreciate it if you didn't tell Marcus any of this. We're not on good terms. I don't want him worrying about me."

She nodded. "He told me about your time off right now."

"Yeah... about that."

"Well do what you need to do. I don't want to keep you any longer."

Raine appreciated her. She was just so whiplashed by her feelings toward this woman since the beginning of their short time knowing each other. But she knew that Lilly also didn't quite care for Jensen either, and was probably upset that he was let off so easy. Raine caught an inkling of that from her when they were talking. She also wondered if perhaps they'd sit down some day together and Raine would hear her story.

The story of why she too, hated the professor.

SEVEN

Raine Walsh

Raine tightened her grip on the wheel. She kept looking from her speedometer to the road and back again. The nerves were all too familiar as she sped to get there. Of course, the thought of getting pulled over by police, or even getting into a wreck came to mind, but she couldn't get the long road or the destination ahead out of her focus.

However, she kept thinking that everything Jensen was doing was to get to her, so he'd wait for her before doing anything irrational. That was really the only thought that brought her comfort. And that in itself was disturbing. She called Arie to let him know that she secured the address from Lilly and was headed that way. She also texted him the ad-dress, so that he would have it.

Driving down the highway, she hoped her hunch was correct that he'd taken her there—if it was even him at all. Though just as she was beginning to zone out on the long stretch of highway, her phone rang. It came up as an un-known number.

She couldn't take any chances, so she answered the phone, and held it up to her ear as she was driving. If this was a telemarketer, she was going to be pissed. "Hello?"

"Raine." Her heart pinged in her chest at the sound of the weak voice.

"Chloe!" She began to heave breaths, realizing at once that she was experiencing a panic attack at the sound of her sister's voice. She swerved the car off to the side and checked all mirrors to make sure no other cars were near. She simply couldn't drive in this condition, with her hands shaking and clammy, and her brain closing in on itself, the edges of her vision blackening. She put the car in park on the side of the road. "Are you okay? Are you hurt? Where are you?"

"I only have a minute." She spoke quickly. "I'm here at this… big house. A guy came to your apartment, they wanted you, but you weren't home, they thought I was you."

"Who?" She already knew who.

"Alex was his assistant."

Bingo. The hunch was no longer a hunch.

"I don't know where I am."

"Did you drive for a long time?" she asked.

"Yes."

Raine knew exactly where she was. "Are you hurt?"

"No."

"Chloe, listen to me. I'm already on my way to you, okay? I know where they took you."

"No!" Her voice was aggressive.

Raine felt dumbstruck. Frozen. She didn't know what to do or what to say.

"They want you to do that. He wants you, Raine."

"I know. I've been fighting this battle for some time." She tried to keep her words short and quick.

"He just has me to get to you. Don't come."

"You really think I'm going to listen to that?" She almost thought she heard Chloe laugh, which was crazy considering the situation. "I'm coming, please hang in there. Just, comply. He doesn't want you, but you're valuable because he can use you to get to me, okay? Remember that."

"One more thing, Raine," she said, her voice broken and struck with grief.

"What?"

"He killed Alex. He told me." She sniffled, her voice as weak as it was when Raine first heard it.

She tried to swallow the hard lump in her throat. She imagined him running over the skinny college kid that her sister was in love with. It made her hate him even more.

Nobody listened to her. She knew it was him that killed Alex. She knew.

Her terror quickly turned to anger. "Hang in there. I'm coming. I love you."

"Gotta go!" Chloe screeched into the phone, and then click.

The line went dead.

Raine dropped the phone into the passenger seat and slammed her hands on the wheel several times in anger. The motion did nothing to help and made her hands sting as hot tears rolled down her cheeks.

She could try one last ditch effort to call the one person who was able to help her in the past, even though they were both mad at each other.

It was her last resort.

She was at that point.

EIGHT

Detective Heely

J onah stepped out of his car and closed the door, looking up at the buildings around him. It would have been
smart to look at a map before he came here, and he regretted not doing so immediately. He was too excited at the
lead though, to waste more time before hopping in the car.
With a brand new yellow steno pad and pen, he was eager to
fill its pages so that he could complete his wall puzzle back
home.

As he took a step forward, his phone buzzed in his
pocket. He pulled it out and glanced at the caller ID. "Well,
well, well... speak of the devil," he sang into the phone, re-
gretting it immediately. He didn't want her knowing that he
was thinking about her in any way. *What the hell?* he berated
himself. He could blow his own cover.

"Heely. I need your help." Raine started many a conversation to him this way. "My sister's been kidnapped."

His sly smirk quickly melted from his face as he heard
the urgency and terror in her words through the phone.
"How do you know this?" He couldn't help but blurt out the
question.

"It's a long story—"

It always was.

"—but I just got off the phone with her and it confirmed my fears. She's been taken by Dill Jensen, the professor."

"They've cleared him." He knew this information even though he didn't have anything to do with his case. Raine had been rattling about the guy since the beginning. She had something against him.

"This is different—" she shouted, frantic into the phone.

"Raine!" He cut her off, "I can't help you."

"Then I'll call Jos- Detective Hatch."

"Oh, is that a threat? Move on to the next idiot detective?" he asked. He was ruder to her than he'd thought he would be. He couldn't help his feelings. The emotions were building, and he wasn't prepared for this phone call. He should have let it go to voicemail. But then again, he was also done playing all of her games, no matter what.

"Heely, I don't know what you're talking about."

"I'm at a work thing. Gotta go." He hung up the call and pocketed his cell phone again. A small part of him was weighted by guilt. *What am I doing?* The terror in her voice was something he'd never heard before. She was really worried about her sister. She believed every word she said to him, and was looking for help, something that he was born to do. *To help people. To put bad people away.* She called him, of all people, even when she was mad at him and vice versa, which probably took guts, and he was just a big asshole to her.

But then there was the other side of it.

It could be a trap.

She's been around him long enough to sense and exploit his weaknesses—one being the need to help others and put bad people away. She could be playing into that. And how convenient that it came right when he's a detective again. *No. I'm not going to be tempted to fall into her games.*

He looked up at his beautiful surroundings. Freshly planted red and white flowers strategically placed. The rich look of the terracotta colored buildings with red, Spanish influenced rooftops. The Stanford campus. He was ready to find out more information about the alumni that he was so close with yet knew nothing about. This was the perfect place to start his research, and he actually needed to speak to the professor she had a vendetta against.

Because he knew there was more to the story.

Jonah pulled out the campus map that the administration office gave him. He claimed to be touring the school, which was a great cover because lots of parents and potential students were touring the campus today. He made sure of that before he picked up and got in the car, so that it wouldn't be so obvious he was investigating. People get weird about PI's poking around. They get weird about handing out information, or answering questions, or showing you around. Part of it could be that *they* don't want to be investigated. There was a sense of vulnerability surrounding it. The old 'I'm not going to stick up for you to the bully because then I may be bullied' mentality.

He waited outside the residence hall for the student residence advisor to meet him, to start this assigned tour of the campus. He hoped he was playing this game correctly.

"Jonah, my man!" He heard the voice from behind him, so he spun around to see a burly college kid with blond curly hair and pearly white teeth smiling at him. "Are you my 1:30?" he asked.

"Tour? Uhh yes," he said.

"Now is this for you, or for your kid? I tend to give the tour differently knowing that information."

Jonah laughed unintentionally. He remembered college before the police academy. This kid was the perfect student to be giving tours. The most stereotypical undergrad tour guide they could find. "It's uhh, for me. I know I don't look like your conventional college student. And I'll most definitely commute. But I was thinking about coming back and got accepted here. Now I'm just weighing my options."

"Got it. Well my name is Jordan, if you have any questions along the way. Is there anything in particular you'd like to see, or should I just do a whole comprehensive tour? You certainly don't need the residence hall section if you're commuting."

"Naw, that's all right." He scanned his eyes up and down the high rise that Jordan came out of. "I am rather interested in the psychology department though. I heard it's really good, and I'd love to check out those facilities if that's cool." He tried to add some hip slang in there and not his detective language all the time, so this Jordan guy would trust him.

The kid didn't seem to care. He probably saw all different kinds of people coming through here.

"Oh, all right. We can start over in that department if you'd like. It's a little bit of a walk."

Jordan started off in that direction.

Jonah followed closely behind.

"So, you have a girl friend?" he asked, throwing Jonah completely off guard.

He thought for a moment. He generally was not vocal or obvious about his sexuality and was annoyed that that was even a thing in society, or the fact that this kid asked him if he was with a girl first, without even knowing him. "Naw, dude I'm gay." The words escaped his mouth before he had time to judge them. He caught Jordan side eyeing him with hesitation, probably to see if he was joking or not, and then he responded with a nonchalant, "Right on! Do you have a boyfriend then?"

His words flowed naturally. This guy was good at being social. That's probably why they chose him to be the tour
guide.

Jonah stifled a small laugh. "Not right now. Doing the
solo thing for a little bit. Just got out of a long-term relationship."

"Oh, sorry man."

"No, it's all good!"

"Is that why you're having your midlife crises here?"

That question literally made Jonah laugh out loud,
from the belly. "Is that what you think this is? How old do
you think I am?"

"I'm just joshing with ya." Jordan slapped him on the
back. "We're about there. The main building of the department of psychology. Class isn't in session now, so you're
free to kind of just walk around the building if you'd like,
although all the floors are the same."

Jonah watched as Jordan's attention was taken by a
group of girls giggling by a light post near the entrance to
the building.

"I can just go in then?" Jonah asked, knowing the question was lost on Jordan.

"I've seen it a million times dude, I'll wait right here
for you to come back."

Jonah couldn't help but crack a small smile, as Jordan
didn't even look at him while he said the words. He turned
and entered the building.

Right when he walked in, there was a bulletin board on
the wall that had room numbers and professors' names on it.
Jonah's gaze followed the names until he landed on one he
recognized, because Raine had mentioned it so many times.
He was hoping with everything he had that the professor
was here right now. That would be so great, to get to have a
conversation with him.

He looked behind him to see that Jordan stayed behind, he was clearly distracted with the group of girls, and Jonah pushed through some double doors to the stairs, which he took to the second floor. He walked down the hall and turned at the door. He knocked. No answer.

He looked through the small window into the office. A haze appeared on the other side. He tried the knob. To his surprise, it was unlocked. He looked up and down the hallways before entering the room.

This was pure luck, and he knew it. Nobody was around, so he'd get a chance to poke around this professor's office. Of course, it'd be better if he could speak to the guy himself, but this would have to do. He didn't know where to start, exactly. The office was quite small. It wasn't a classroom, just a closet office, with a desk and bookshelves surrounding the entire room. It smelled of musty paper and old pieces of literature. And Jonah's eyes were attracted to the books on the shelves. They were all psychology related in some way, and it seemed as though this guy was obsessed with history. The history of psych. The history of disease. The history of studying the mind. He moved to the desk and began to shuffle through papers, which looked like essays.

His eyes were specifically attracted to the notes on hypnosis. Jonah knew nothing about hypnosis, only that it was quite the controversial topic. Everything in this room was evidence concerning the case that had just happened, and he wondered if Josie Hatch had gotten her hands on anything in here. It didn't look touched to him. When police had warrants, they usually didn't care about the state they left it in. However, Jonah felt that this office was exactly how the professor left it. It didn't feel tampered with. Perhaps they only checked his home as a crime scene, and because his alibi was so strong, like Raine had told him, they didn't bother checking out the other parts of his life.

But what he didn't understand was why did Raine loathe the guy? Why did she have it out for him? Was he an easy target? Did he give her bad marks in college and she was out for some sort of revenge? Nothing in this office indicated that she existed, which just made the search harder.

"Can I help you?"

The voice from the door made him jump out of his skin. He dropped the papers to the desk and they scattered. He turned around slowly to face the woman leaning against the doorframe.

"You startled me!" he laughed.

"What are you doing in here?" she asked, her face not cracking a smile.

"I'm a..." he tried to think of a good excuse. Just stick with the one you came here with! "I'm touring the university. I have an interest in psychology. This door was open. I was hoping to speak with a few professors on their opinion of the program. Is this your office?" He already knew the answer.

"This is Professor Jensen's office. Mine is down the hall. It's quiet around this time, so the shuffling inside here threw me off. Jensen's not here right now, so I was surprised when I heard the commotion and came to check it out. What did you say your name was?"

"Jonah," he croaked. He hadn't thought of a cover name before coming here. Nobody knew him. He didn't think he'd need it.

"You're..." Her eyes narrowed. "You're that detective."

He was completely caught off guard, almost as though her words slammed him into the dusty bookcases behind him. "What?" was the only thing he could think of to say.

"Sorry... I uhh, let me introduce myself," she said.

"Please do."

"My name is Dr. Lilly Everstien. I'm a professor of psychology here. However, I work part time in a clinical therapist's office..."

He already knew who she was before she'd finished her introduction. "With Raine Walsh and Marcus Altor," he finished.

She smiled. "And you're that detective I've heard so much about."

He didn't know where her allegiance lay.

"And we shouldn't be speaking inside this office, where you don't belong. Let's go back to mine and chat a moment." She was calm.

He felt like a dog that was in trouble, with his tail between his legs. The hardest thing was that he didn't know whether or not to trust this lady. He would play it cool. This could be a good thing.

He followed her to her office, then plopped down on the chair opposite her desk. She leaned against her desk in her tight pencil skirt, her skinny legs poking out the bottom.

"Eyes up here, buddy." she said, motioning a poke at her own eyes with her middle and index finger before crossing her arms over her chest.

"No offense, you're not my type." He stifled a laugh. "So, what's this 'you've heard a lot about me?'"

She nodded. "Mostly through Marcus. Raine's been preoccupied lately with all the shit she's been going through. He says you two, you and Raine got in a tiff. Aren't on good terms."

It was Jonah's turn to nod. But he didn't much feel like really going deep into that topic.

"I was happy when I heard rustling in that office, because I thought you were Jensen, and that would have been good news."

Jonah contemplated that. "Oh yeah?" Raine's story about Jensen kidnapping her sister and taking her to another state seemed farfetched, but maybe he was onto something now with this Lilly woman. "Why would that be good?"

"Because if he was here... that means he couldn't be there."

"What do you mean?" The mood in the room grew sinister.

"You know what I'm talking about."

He studied her face a moment. What did she know that he couldn't pick up on? "You're going to need to elaborate on that."

"Come on, Jonah. I know you're not stupid. And I know that Raine went to you for help. And you didn't believe her. So now she's gone off on her own to see if she can get her sister back."

The air in the room grew thin and suddenly it was hard for him to breathe. "Do you... believe her?" he asked quietly, hesitantly.

"I don't know. I didn't want her going there alone if that's what you mean. She said she had some sort of backup though. And obviously Jensen isn't here. And nobody knows what he's capable of. But there's a lot of talk around here that they let him off without fully checking the facts. He has some sort of leverage."

"Do you know the address of where she went?"

Lilly stood from the desk and walked around it, staring out the window. "I'm not sure if it'll break my trust with her."

"Lilly! If this is true, and she's in danger, I don't know what I'd do with the fact that I simply ignored her cry for help." The thought of the phone call he shared with her not that long ago was ringing in his head. He wasn't sure anyone could fake the emotions he sensed in her voice. Also, perhaps he should be tailing her to keep tabs on her. He certainly didn't want her leaving the state when so much was at stake.

"I know the address," she said quietly. "I gave it to Raine."

"Well give it to me!" he shouted, becoming impatient.

They stared each other in the eyes a moment, and then she nodded and scrawled it down on a post-it note, allowing him to release a huge exhale he'd been holding inside for too long.

NINE

Raine Walsh

Raine was numb from head to toe, and drove because she had to, terrified at where the directions were taking her. It'd been hours, and she had to stop for gas once, looking over her shoulders and staying fully alert. Her eyes itched with fatigue.

So many thoughts crossed her mind, and she thought out every scenario. If Jensen had only taken Chloe to get to her, why would he take her across state lines? Was it because of his case in the Bay Area? Or the fact that his house had been under surveillance for some time? He could possibly be afraid that he was being tailed, even though he was cleared, and it wasn't entirely suspicious that he'd go to his vacation home in Arizona.

As she drove, she worried even more that she had to turn on her headlights. The sun was setting on the horizon, the sky settling into a deeper blue. The darkness brought more uncertainty.

It became apparent as she turned off on a side road that went on for ages through what seemed like nothing but desert, that this place she was driving to would be fairly secluded. She cursed at every yawn, because she would need all her strength and awareness to be able to make smart decisions in front of the professor.

Whenever a reflective green sign appeared in the distance, she'd become mesmerized. It looked as though the reflective mile markers were floating on the deepening blue and purple horizon. She rubbed at her eyes and hit the gas.

It was only then, that she realized the GPS had her turning in to a driveway. She thought it was another road, considering she couldn't see what it led to. As she looked down at her phone, it indicated she had reached her destination, and this is where the directions ended.

She texted Arie, *I made it. Haven't gone in yet.* And waited a moment to see if he'd respond. Her head nearly hit the ceiling of the car when the phone vibrated in her lap, and the house came into view as she drove down the driveway.

She didn't know whether or not to look at the responding text, to take her eyes off the house. She pulled over to the side and turned off all the lights in the car, sitting in the dark in the driveway. She looked at the text.

Wasn't able to follow. Be safe. I love you.

She sat, stunned by the message.

For multiple reasons.

For one, Arie wasn't behind her, and wasn't able to explain the reason for that right now. That meant she was completely and entirely alone. Before, she had the security of knowing that somebody was there to swoop in if she was in deep trouble. Now she was definitely alone.

But that wasn't the thing that stunned her the most. He'd said the L word. The three-word sentence that not even she and Marcus had said. And to her, seeing those words, even though it was a text, filled her with so much more than she ever could have imagined. It was exactly what she needed to hear before working up the courage to do what she had to do to save her sister.

And she decided to respond, *I do, too.* She pocketed her phone, and left Chloe's sitting on the passenger seat. She shut off the car and pocketed the keys as well.

She looked up at the mansion. It was one of those typical vacation homes in Arizona, set back from the road, palm trees and accent lighting all around. Surely there was a huge, lighted, inground pool in the back.

She could sneak into the house, but she had no clue what the floor plan of this place was or where he could possibly be holding her sister. The easiest and quickest way to get to him was to do it the old-fashioned way. Ring the doorbell.

Where she had been tired before, she was wide awake now as she put one foot in front of the other and walked through the rocks to get to the front door. The path was decorative rocks instead of grass. She inched up the steps and looked to the side of the door for a doorbell.

Even though she'd had all that time in the car driving here, she did not even remotely know what to say, or what to re-hearse for this moment. The porch light flicked on before she heard the gears of the locks turning. The breath caught in her throat.

"You came."

Raine was taken aback by the person who answered the door, as it wasn't who she thought it'd be. It was not the professor. It was nobody other than the skinny, blonde haired sister she'd been rushing to save, standing there, untouched, looking in better shape than Raine.

Without thinking, Raine threw her arms around her sister and embraced her hard, tears welling up in her eyes. She was alive. She wasn't hurt. She wasn't in chains. She was standing right in front of her. And she... answered the door. If she had access to the door— why didn't she run in the first place?

"Chloe, are you hurt?" she whispered into her ear.

"No."

"Let's get out of here. I have a car parked right outside."

"No!" she yelled.

Raine backed up and grabbed the side of her face, feeling as though her eardrum almost burst at her sister's cry. "What the hell?" She was still speaking softly. Who was this girl in front of her? She was *not* acting normal. "What's going on?" she asked, not knowing what else she could do.

And then her heart skipped a beat as the man emerged from the door. The same white hair, the same skinny glasses perched on his crooked nose. The same sly smile.

She backed up at the sight of him, grabbing Chloe's arm.

"Welcome, Raine Walsh. How nice of you to join us." His voice was calm, and half amused. "You must be exhausted from your trip."

"Shut up. Don't talk to me like nothing is wrong. You kidnapped my sister!" she yelled, knowing how ridiculous and immature it sounded, but it was her stone-cold reality.

The professor crossed his arms over his chest, a look of amusement on his face. "You came all this way, might as well come in for a chat," he said calmly.

Raine boiled up inside. The pressure in her head was pounding, and her eye began to twitch with frustration. She looked from Chloe back to the professor, and over his shoulder into the house to see if anyone else was possibly there.

"Just... listen to him, sis." Chloe smiled.

It wasn't a real smile, and perhaps Chloe was so scared all she could do was comply. Raine understood Stockholm Syndrome, but she also wasn't going to give this guy the satisfaction. If he'd been watching her as closely as she thought he had, he would know she was a fighter if nothing else.

"No!" she yelled at her sister. "Come on, Chloe! This dirty old man killed Alex! Who knows what else he did?"

He stepped forward.

Raine stepped back.

"You will come into this house. You will have a conversation with me. And then you and your sister may go on your way."

She remembered that it sounded the way it did when she was in trouble in his class all those years ago. He was good at manipulation, but Chloe's strategy of compliance might be the only thing she could do now. He made it sound like if Raine didn't listen to him, there would be consequences. And there was no help out here. She and Chloe were on their own.

Reluctantly, she stepped over the threshold into the grand entryway. She wondered, momentarily, how being a professor, he'd acquired so much wealth—between his house back in the Bay Area, and this vacation home here.

"I'd like to speak with you alone, without your sister here."

"Well you brought her here." Raine shot back, her eyes glazed over.

"Chloe, you go into this room over here, and I will take Raine into my office to speak. We'll come back for you afterwards."

She nodded, and Raine watched as she crossed the foyer into the room he'd guided her to. It was some sort of sitting area.

She went inside.

Jensen pulled the door closed, then locked it.

Raine swallowed hard.

He was being cordial, almost nice even. But there was still the intuition of creepy. The keys. Locking Chloe in the room. She was going to stay on her guard the entire time. And even though she was getting more tired by the minute, she *had* to stay on her guard.

"We're going to go down the hall and to your right."

He was behind her, and she put one foot in front of the other. She'd worked herself up into a fury, using anger to fuel her courage. There were so many things wrong with this situation. So many memories of her time at Stanford were coming up in her mind. Walking to his office after she'd had to fight for her grade in his class. The inappropriate behavior he exhibited toward her when she thought he would be a professor she could trust and reach out to. He wasn't. And because of him, her trust had changed from that point on. Within the short walk down the hall to the room he'd pointed her to, she thought about what it was that led her to this point.

She walked into the room. It was an office, nothing odd about it. Books lined the walls, a sitting area in the middle. Four stiff armchairs pointed at each other around a coffee table.

"Would you like a drink?" he asked.

She shook her head. "No." She wasn't about to consume anything from him.

"You're my guest, so I thought I'd offer."

She thought for a moment. Every response needed to be calculated, because he'd be analyzing it as well. "I'm fine," she lied. She sure could use a drink of water.

"I'm going to have to ask you one more thing."

Her stomach wrenched. *Oh great... here we go.*

"While you're here, you're going to need to give me that cell phone in your pocket."

Her lifeline. Her only lifeline back to Arie, her back up. "I'd rather not."

"You have no choice." He smiled, his pointed incisors visible. She'd never noticed that before. She'd never managed to stare at his face for too long.

"There are others that know I'm here. If I don't respond when they message me, they'll come after me."

"Who, Lilly? What is that little mouse going to do to help you and your sister, hm?"

Raine burned inside.

"Oh, you didn't think I knew where you got this address? It was the obvious choice for planting. I knew you'd run to her first."

It was as though he was always one step ahead of her. "Not just Lilly."

"Hand it over. I'll make sure they are informed of your... safety."

She didn't trust him. Not one bit. But she was also cornered. She didn't want to know what would happen if she didn't give him her phone. She'd have to find another way out. She had before, and she would again. She reached in her pocket and threw the phone to his feet.

He chuckled, bent down and picked it up, then placed it in the breast pocket of his button down shirt.

"What are you going to do to me?" she asked. The words escaped her lips before she had time to think about them.

He stepped into her personal space quicker than she expected and placed a hand on her shoulder.

She leaped back once more. "Don't touch me," she said through gritted teeth.

The look of amusement on his face did not falter. "I've told you. I just want to have a little chat. Sit."

That last word was more of a command than an offer.

She walked over to the armchair on the other side of the table and sat down.

He followed and sat across from her in the other armchair, then crossed one leg over the other.

She sat on the edge of her seat. She didn't want to feel comfortable here. "Why couldn't you just have a conversation with me back in the Bay Area? Why did you have to involve my sister? Why did you make me come all the way out here?"

"Chloe was really quite an accident, if you'll believe me." He laughed. "I sent someone else to go retrieve you, and they brought her back. I was almost fooled when I first saw her... and then when the sedation wore off and she opened her mouth, I knew he'd brought me the wrong girl."

Raine pursed her lips as she listened.

"Then I realized I could use her to get to you."

"I figured as much. Why do you wan—"

"Enough." He put up his hand to quiet her. "I'm the one that will be asking the questions." He leaned back in the chair. "I've waited a long time for this moment with you."

She didn't quite understand the context of his words. But she listened, because that's what he wanted her here for.

"I know everything about you, Raine Walsh. Everything you've been through. I've always been interested in your spirit. So... determined. So stubborn." He smiled. "And with every passing test, you pulled me in more."

Test?... At first she thought he'd meant when she was back in school. A literal sit down and write an essay or fill in the little answer bubbles test. But then the thought occurred to her that perhaps he was talking about something more. She wanted to ask him what he meant by that, but she was afraid to speak. Her limbs were tingling in a way that made her feel as though she'd begin shaking, but she needed to be strong. She'd been through worse than having a conversation with an old professor.

"The truth of the matter is, I've been watching you since you came into my life your freshman year at the university."

That was an unnerving and uncomfortable statement.

"When you refused acceptance into my organization to the alumni psychological club I had formed, I knew that one day I'd be able to show you how important it is that you are a part of it. And when you escaped from Allen, I was drawn to you even more."

She tensed in her seat. "If you knew, why didn't you help me?" she whispered.

He smiled again. "I know you are confused and that you have a lot of questions for me. But you will learn in due time. It must be the right moment, at the right time."

She had no idea what he was talking about.

"What you don't understand, is that I can help you *now*. This entire time, nobody would believe you, Raine. You've been so alone."

Yeah, nobody believed me that you're a psycho, she thought.

"Did you ever stop to think about the fact that you are not so different from those people who tested you? You are not that much different from the situations you've found yourself in, in the last several years?"

She sat back in the chair and absorbed that sentence. The last several years. When her world was shaken by the car wreck and waking up in the nightmare prison. When she'd woken in the hospital because she'd leapt off a skyscraper. When she found herself pinned to the wall in Vinnie's house with his murderous eyes boring down on her, holding a gun that she didn't own or know how to use. When she'd seen the bloody sight of her client Tanner, who'd just escaped a nightmare of his own in the basement of the professor's house, and she'd gotten there too late.

"They were all students of mine. Alumni."

The sentence hit her, though she still had a hard time grasping what he meant.

"Just like you. And just like you, they'd tried to es-cape a reality that just wasn't possible, because it was them. You're the only one who stayed in the field you graduated in, and pursued psychology outside of your education. Yet, are you really able to help others when you haven't been able to help yourself?"

He was right. She couldn't stand to look him in the face. She tried to stay above the conscious level where she knew he was manipulative and could harness power, even with only his words. But he was absolutely right. She hadn't been able to help others, the one thing she'd set out to do. Marcus even made her leave the job because she wasn't succeeding.

She was reminded once again of the client she'd lost to suicide, and how she wasn't able to help him either. He'd come to her for help and she failed him. Everyone she'd set out to help, she'd failed. Why was she doing what she was doing? Wasn't it causing more harm than good?

She couldn't help the single drop that collected at her tear duct and spilled over, down her cheek. "What do you want?" she asked her voice low and weak.

"I want you to partner with me on the greatest psychological study humanity has ever seen."

She was taken aback. She had no idea what that meant.

"For years I've been trying to conduct the study. I've recruited students, alumni, and one after the other they've been eliminated. But you, you remain. For some reason, after all these years, you still manage to escape. You're not doing what your calling is to do, Raine. You are wasting your time. Your life. But if you join me, you could become one of the greatest psychologists the history books have ever seen. I've tried with other students—"

"You murdered Alex Wood," she said quietly, wiping her tears with the back of her hand, her bloodshot eyes staring directly at him.

"He was a threat to the experiment." Jensen whispered. "I wouldn't tell just anyone that. Only you."

"Because you were let off."

"Imagine that."

Those last two words were spoken with such a sinister tone, that it sunk Raine into the ground. Every muscle in her body tensed. Professor Dill Jensen was capable of murder, and she'd just gotten a confession. Though the hard reality of it was that she was in this room with him, and nobody else was here to hear it. Nobody else, just like it had been so far, would believe anything she had to say.

Though something else intrigued her. And that was his proposal. This big psychological study he'd been working on for years. He was choosing her to help him. This opened her mind to so many more questions. *Why me?* He'd said it was because of her perseverance throughout the years. And he knew everything she'd been through, or so he made it sound. She was curious what the experiment entailed. For her, it wasn't about the fame of being the best psychologist in the world. That had never been her goal. But she did choose psychology because she felt she could help others, that had always been her ultimate goal. And Jensen was right. She'd done more harm than good in her attempts to do good. Perhaps clinical psychology was not her calling, like she thought it was. Perhaps she was destined for something much, much bigger. And just like the studies from the past that she'd researched and studied over and over again, though unethical as they may have been in some instances, they all had a lesson to teach about humanity. There was something good that came out of all of them. That was where her interest lay.

She looked into professor Jensen's face for truth. She was a reader of emotions, of human behavior, of trust in her intuition.

"You're tired," he said, his voice soothing. "When one is tired…"

She looked away from his gaze.

"Raine. Look at me."

She snapped back.

"When one is tired, they become highly suggestible. But the choice is entirely yours."

She felt as though her body was numb. She couldn't move, not even her arm to scratch a twitch on her eyelid. She felt trapped by his words, his movements.

"I want to add one last thing to the deal."

She didn't want to listen anymore, but she couldn't stop. How could she even consider this after the amount of hate she'd felt for this man in front of her? What he'd put her through?

"I have given my life to this work. This research. Once we complete the experiment, I give you permission…"

She held onto his every word.

"…to kill me."

"I'm in." She looked at him, wide-eyed, her voice quivering, and she wasn't entirely sure what she was doing. But for some odd, out of this world reason, she felt like this was right. She thought she saw him smile, but just slightly. *What was the catch?* Was he dying from some disease anyway and pawning this experiment off on her was his dying wish?

Regardless of the catch, she hated the man. She loved the psychological research, especially if it resulted in helping people.

"I'm going to let you and your sister leave, but not tonight."

She jumped to protest that, but something told her not to.

"You're exhausted, look at you. You will stay here, as my guest, not as my prisoner. If we are going to be working together, we need to trust each other. I'm going to give you back your phone, unlock your sister's door, and place my keys on a hook by the front door. You have access to whatever you'd like, and you may leave at any time, because I trust you. But—"

There was always a *but*. She waited. *Here's the catch.*

"In the coming days, you must prove to me that you trust me too, and that you can work with me."

"How do I do that?"

"That is for you to figure out. And you're smart. I trust you will have no problem doing that, once you've absorbed and thought about everything we've discussed inside these four walls." He raised his hands to signify the office they sat in.

He reached in his pocket and placed her cell phone on the table between them.

She looked down at it carefully before reaching forward and grabbing it. "What... will I tell everyone?"

"That you were mistaken."

She listened.

"You will tell them that Chloe came here because she was distressed about Alex, and she was confused when I was cleared because she thought I murdered him. But it was a delusion."

Raine nodded.

"And when you came here, you picked her up, stayed the night because you were tired, and then left in the morning."

"Sounds... good."

"Well, Dr. Walsh, I look forward to our partnership." He stood up, waited a moment, and then exited the room.

She continued to sit in the armchair and held her cell phone up to her chest. At that point she allowed herself to exhale all the breath she'd held during the conversation.

There was so much to take in and she didn't know exactly how to process all the information. She didn't know what it was about their conversation, or how she was able to get rid of the anger to actually give him a chance to speak, but there was something inside her, a foreign feeling, a spark of excitement for what might lie ahead.

TEN

Raine Walsh

Before heading back to be with Chloe, she dialed Arie's number.

"Raine, are you okay?"

"Oh, it's good to hear your voice." She smiled.

"I'm okay. Everything's okay."

"Thank god," he breathed. "What the hell is going on? Is Chloe safe? Are you coming back?"

"We're going to spend the night here—"

"What?"

"Wait, babe, hold on, let me explain. I blew things so out of proportion." She could not fathom why, deep inside her, she felt the urge to lie to him, somebody she'd just said she loved. "He didn't kidnap Chloe. She was so distressed about Alex, like you thought. She was having delusions, as was I, obviously, that Jensen killed him, but that wasn't the case. Why would the police let him go with no charges if he'd murdered someone? I've been crazy."

"You... hate using that word." His voice was accusatory.

"Crap, you're right. I'm just so tired from the long drive and everything. I'll explain everything later, perhaps on the drive home tomorrow. I promise. Everything's okay, and I'm coming home to you tomorrow, okay?"

"I don't know... Raine. You seem okay... but also different."

"How could I be the same, Arie, after what you said to me just earlier? I can't get it out of my head." She leaned forward on the chair, the phone pressed into her ear so hard that it was beginning to heat her ear.

He stifled a small laugh. "I just wish that it was in person and not a text. But regardless, it felt right, Raine. And I meant it. And I want you to be safe."

"Well you can say it to me tomorrow in person when I'm home, okay?"

"Deal."

"Goodnight, Arie."

"Seriously, text or call if you need anything or feel comfortable. I'm here for you."

"I know. Night." She hung up. A strange calm blanketed her, and she wanted to go see her sister.

As she left the office, she heard voices coming from down the hall. Professor Jensen came out of the room he'd locked Chloe in earlier, and she stopped in her tracks as he looked up at her.

"She's already asleep," he whispered.

Raine found that odd, but perhaps she'd worn herself out.

"I just went ahead and put blankets and a few pillows in there for you guys since that's where she is. If you want, there are several bedrooms upstairs, and you're welcome to any of those beds. I just didn't want to touch her while she was sleeping on the couch."

Raine nodded. "Thank you.

He nodded in return, and then turned and walked up the stairs.

She stood in the dark foyer until he was out of sight, and then made for the room in the front. Sure enough, Chloe was curled up in a ball on the couch in front of the big windows.

She closed the door and locked it, even though she was aware that the ring of keys was just outside the door, and of course Jensen could come in if he wanted. She didn't think he would, but the vulnerability of sleeping made her feel more secure with a locked door. She tiptoed back over to the couch and knelt down on the floor by the pillows that lay there. She grabbed a crocheted quilt and laid it over her sister's body. Then she stroked her blond hair with the palm of her hand.

Chloe shook awake, her eyes wide.

"Shh." Raine said, feeling guilty that she'd woken her.

"Raine? What's going on—"

"Shh, it's okay, Chloe. Go back to sleep. We're safe."

"We're safe? What happened?"

"Nothing happened. We're going to rest here and leave in the morning."

Chloe sat up on her elbows and looked at Raine with squinted, studious eyes, as though she were studying her for signs of information that she was not telling her. "Oh my god... did you kill him?" she whispered.

Raine covered her mouth, worried that her laugh would be too loud. "No, of course not! We had a conversation and clarified a lot of confusion that I'd been feeling," she said. "I'm unable to explain everything now, but I can explain on the way back home tomorrow."

"Why did he kidnap me?" she whined, almost child-like, a quiver in her voice, a look of confusion in her eyes.

"It was the only way he could have a conversation with me. I'm sorry that had to happen to you. I just, wouldn't give him the time of day before, and it was very important that we got the chance to speak, like we did tonight. But everything's okay and I want you to get a good sleep after this stressful day, okay?"

Chloe nodded, her eyelids drooping as she laid her head back down. "I'm glad... everything's okay," she slurred as she closed her eyes once more.

Raine laid the other pillow and blanket on the floor next to the couch. She could have explored upstairs, but she didn't want to leave her sister. The floor would have to be okay for now. She took the car keys out of her pocket and put them on the floor next to her phone, and then lay her head down. She traced the shadowed lines on the floor reflected from the window frames in the moonlight.

Her mind moved a million miles a minute and she didn't think there was any possibility of rest, but she closed her eyes anyway and listened to her breathing. Perhaps she could meditate herself to sleep, just like she had in the prison, which felt like so long ago. Oftentimes, she recalled situations where she needed to coax herself into doing something when her mind refused.

She didn't know if the choices she was making were right, or if they would pan out the way she'd envisioned them. All that seemed important was protecting Chloe and protecting Arie in whatever way the situation would allow.

It was survival mode. Only this wasn't a physical fight. This was a fight of the mind.

ELEVEN

Raine Walsh

She woke to a tap on her arm, which shook her.

"It's just me."

She heard the words whispered from a soft, sweet voice. Her eyelids fluttered open to see her bright-eyed sister above her.

"Sorry to wake you, but let's get outta here." Chloe whispered.

Raine rubbed at her eyes and sat up, then leaned against the couch. She'd had a dreamless night. It was as though she'd just closed her eyes. It was still rather dark outside, with just a small bit of light blue sky only beginning to emerge at its edges.

"What time is it?" she slurred. Her back hurt, surely from sleeping on the floor. It wasn't the most comfortable arrangement, but considering their situation, it could have been much worse.

"Just going on five."

"Geeze Chloe, when have you ever been known to rise early?" She was only half joking.

"I don't wanna be here longer than we have to. I just want to get back, you know?"

Raine nodded. "Yes, I agree." She rubbed her eyes again and rolled onto her knees to push herself to standing.

"How do we get out of here?"

"The front door."

Chloe was quiet a moment. "You mean we can just leave?" she asked, astounded.

"Yes, he's not keeping us here. At this point, we're his guests."

"Raine, be straight with me. What did you do to allow this?" she asked, whispering, and looking around the room as though they were being watched.

She felt the question deep down inside her gut, and it made her squirm. "Nothing. I haven't done—I'm not... entirely sure yet. But I know that we're not prisoners, okay? Whatever you thought happened to Alex... didn't." That last sentence was a complete lie. The professor flat out told her that Alex had to go because he was interfering with the integrity of the experiment. Of course that terrified her, but she understood the ramifications of Chloe knowing this information.

"Can we just go? This place gives me the creeps."

Raine nodded. "Yeah okay." She followed her sister, who unlocked the room and walked to the front door. Quietly, she opened the front door and slipped out. Raine looked up toward the grand staircase a moment and realized she had a lot to think about. Then she walked out of the house into the warm, dry, Arizona air.

"Whose car is that?" Chloe asked.

"It's actually Arie's neighbor's." Raine laughed. "You want to drive since you're so awake?"

Chloe laughed. "Okay."

Raine tossed her the keys and then rounded the car to the passenger side. She opened the door and picked up Chloe's phone off the passenger seat. "Oh hey, I brought this for you."

"Oh. Thank you."

"See, that's when I knew you'd left in a hurry." Raine said. "You never go anywhere without this thing."

"Yeah, I'd been really distressed about... Alex." Her voice was muffled as she bit her lip, as though it were painful to say his name.

As Chloe illuminated the headlights and pulled out of the driveway, Raine thought back to the conversation that happened the night before.

She thought about her mission upon leaving that house. She needed to prove in some way, her loyalty to the work that she was going to engage in with the professor.

Did she only agree to work with him because she felt like it was her only way out? Out of the nightmare of having him in her life? She was no murderer, but the thought of a world without Dill Jensen brought her so much relief. She would never be safe with him around.

There was still a part of her that knew she didn't have the whole story from him. And it didn't help to think that he'd followed her over the years, through everything she'd endured. Was that his *only* involvement over the years as an observer—or did he play a more active role? How could he?

What exactly was the club that he'd wanted to recruit her into since she was in college? Could it be that he was trying to draft who would work best to work on this revolutionary psychological study? He told her she was not much different than the demons that haunted her... and that was the most troubling thing to think about of all.

"Raine?"

She snapped out of her trance. "Hm?"

"You okay?"

The delicateness of her sister's voice was far beyond her usual maturity. Of course, her sister had grown up over the last few months.

She smiled. "Yes, just tired," she lied. It was a good one though since it was so early in the morning. "But I can't wait to get back and see Vi and Arie."

"Viona!" Chloe shouted.

Raine smiled again. "She's okay. I had to go out and find her, and she's the reason I smell the way I do—"

"I wasn't going to say anything." She laughed.

"I'm sorry that those people thought you were me and dragged you into this." She wasn't even entirely sure *who* showed up at her door, took Chloe, and let Viona out. Jensen said that he'd sent someone else.

"Do things like this often happen to you when you have colleagues that want to speak with you?"

"No, but this situation is weird because Jensen had been in the spotlight, carefully watched by law enforcement, and he wanted to lay low."

"I thought you hated that man. Just a few months ago you were pissed at me for dating someone who was even slightly associated with him."

"I know. I don't *not* hate him still."

"Hm." Chloe finished. It was as though she wanted to say something more, but she held her tongue.

Raine didn't press the matter. She didn't want to talk about it anyway. She was already deceiving one of the people she was the closest to. And just the fact that Jensen had indeed killed Alex because he was going to ruin the psychological research. Chloe didn't know that. She thought she did, but somehow Jensen was able to convince her that she was just in despair about losing her lover that she was wanted to blame anyone. There was no proof and nobody was charged for it. It was just a tragic hit and run.

That was troubling for Raine. She had already begun to dig a hole below the line of trust with the ones she most trusted, out of fear that Jensen was watching and could pull the plug on their whole agreement. The stakes of that happening put her actions and words at a lot of risk.

The most troubling thing of all, that kept her mind wheeling for the rest of the drive, was the fact that she needed to prove to Jensen that she was loyal to the work. And she wasn't sure how to achieve that. And somehow, she knew that he was the type of person that would know whether or not she'd followed through, and the type of person to not let it go if she hadn't.

It was a dangerous game.

What in the world did she just sign up for?

TWELVE

Detective Heely

Jonah pulled into the driveway of the tall brownstone that had gained so much attention over the past several weeks. The house had been a crime scene for a little while, though police were finished with it. The house and the homeowner were cleared, since nobody was found dead on the property, just injured with some weird shit going on between students in the basement. They'd apparently had access to the house while Jensen was away on vacation.

He sat in the car a moment, looking down at his yellow lined steno pad, his notes scrawled across the page. Before he took off down to this guy's vacation home, if he was even going to do that, he needed to see if he was at home. Upon leaving Stanford and his conversation with Lilly, he was feeling the urge to rush right to the address she'd written on a scrap of paper for him. But something wasn't right about that. Something deep inside told him to cover his bases before he made that decision. He'd made too many mistakes as of late, and he wasn't going to start his private work off on the wrong foot.

He still wasn't fully trusting of Raine. And if he was going to get any more information on her, he'd need to talk to the professor. At least this professor could speak to how she was as a student. The guy was also really well respected in the community of psychology, and he might know her as a professional as well, or know others in the profession that he could refer an investigator to.

What if he'd rushed all the way down to that vacation home when the professor had been at his primary residence the entire time?

Jonah locked his car, then made his way to the front door. He looked back and forth to make sure nobody was around. He knew that reporters could be lurking, waiting for him to come out, though enough time had passed since the case that they appeared to all be gone. He knocked on the door, wondering whether or not he should have conjured up a cover story. Perhaps Jensen hearing that he was a private eye would scare him off. But he wasn't really here to discuss anything concerning Dill Jensen, he was there to discuss the girl that connected them.

He stepped back and waited. This was ultimately the scariest part of his job, in his opinion. The cold calls. People were always so wary of detectives. It was comforting to remember that nothing he wore physically indicated he was one. Back when he worked for the police force, it was probably worse and more intimidating. But now, cold calls were just out of place because nobody did the door to door thing anymore.

And by nobody, not just police or detectives. The world had shifted. Now if somebody was knocking at your door, it was because you were expecting them. The age of technology had done that to society. And if you weren't expecting them, why were they there to begin with?

Nobody came up to the door because they were lost. Rarely did people come to the door as traveling salesmen. The world had just changed over the years.

He leaned forward and knocked again. After all, it was a big house. Perhaps the knock was unheard? When nobody answered that time, he heaved a big sigh. Perhaps the guy wasn't home. That wouldn't stop him from trying. Jonah backed off the porch and looked around again.

The neighborhood was fairly quiet. The houses were pretty close together, as were most in the Bay Area, but there was still enough residential greenery that there tended to be cover.

He listened a moment and heard a lawn mower in the distance, though it seemed to be coming from the back. Perhaps that was Jensen mowing the lawn? Judging by his house and the way his office was, he didn't appear to be a lawn guy, though it could also be the neighbor. It wouldn't hurt to make his way to the back and take a peek.

He hopped down the stairs and crossed the walk, through the grass to the side of the house. He looked over the fence into an in ground pool, the accent lighting making Jonah envious. The mower appeared to be from the house behind Jensen's brownstone.

"Can I help you?"

The voice startled him, and right away he cursed himself for not being more aware. Perhaps the droning sound of the lawn mower put him in a haze. His attention fell to the bald man that sat in a lawn chair outside of Jensen's brownstone. "Forgive me, sir! I was knocking at the front door but nobody answered. My name is Detective Heely." It slipped. So much for the cover story.

The man shifted, and Jonah put his hands in front of him in defense.

"Before you turn off, please know that I am not here to discuss anything about the cases that just concluded. You must be Dr. Dill Jensen?" he asked.

The man smiled.

It made Jonah squirm inside seeing his crooked, yellow teeth. He felt bad for judging, but he just figured the guy would look more professional considering his stature, perhaps more social looking, although who was he to decide what the guy should look like? The man was supposed to be a genius. "I just came to speak to you about—"

"I'm not Dill." The man said in a nasally voice.

That took Jonah aback. *Well why didn't he say so sooner?* "Oh, I'm sorry. I thought since this was his residence... this *is* his residence, right?"

"Yeah, but I'm just watching it for him. He's not home."

"Oh, okay." Of course, Jensen wasn't here. He was at the vacation home, waiting for Raine. Jonah didn't believe this professor would flee so soon after his cases. But then again, there was nothing keeping him from not going. "Would you mind telling me when he'll be back?"

"If you don't mind me telling him you were poking around."

Jonah was caught off guard. The man's smiled turned completely off, and the bags under his eyes set a tone that sent chills down his spine. This man was *not* joking around. "I'm sorry, I must be mistaken. Is that a threat?" He was the one here to ask questions.

"Yes." The man answered.

Jonah straightened and backed from the fence. "You don't intimidate me."

"I should."

Geeze, who IS this guy? "You have a good day." Jonah nodded to him. This conversation was over. He could see he wasn't going to get anywhere, and he didn't necessarily feel like chatting with this man to begin with, especially if he wasn't Jensen. He made his way back to the car.

When he sat inside the car, he locked the door and looked back up at the brownstone. Was it just him, or was the job more and more taxing these days? It was like he couldn't get any wins. He needed to do something to break the routine. Perhaps he was just too engulfed in it, and he needed to take a step back to gain clarity.

Life had been lonely lately.

Perhaps he needed a night out. Though if that were the case, he was going to need to go back to his apartment to clean up first. Even if only to metaphorically wash the work off of him before he went out. First things first, he needed to get out of that creep's driveway.

And as he looked in his rearview mirror and began to pull out, he looked back at the house once more to imagine the horror that went on inside that basement. As he drove away, he could have sworn he saw the curtains in the front window rustle. The two eyes were there one moment, and then they were gone.

THE DOMINO EFFECT

THIRTEEN

Detective Heely

Jonah closed his eyes and the water streamed down his face and chest. Upon turning, the high-pressured shower beamed on his neck and upper back. He inhaled deeply, breathing in the soothing steam and allowed the work to roll off his body and swirl down the drain.

He grabbed his body wash and dispensed a generous amount into the palm of his hand, then rubbed them together. The scent of bergamot and citrus wafted and he rubbed the soap in his hair, lathering it into a foam. Then he used his palms to bring the soap down and around his face, covering the overgrown beard that masked his clean cut jawline. With his eyes closed, he reached over to the built-in shelf and felt around a few soaps and shampoo bottles for his razor.

Stroke by stroke, he rid himself of the facial hair that symbolized his laziness, and his lack of meticulous care of his appearance. He *did* care. Just so much in his life had been hectic recently, that he chose to allow himself to fall to the wayside. And he was done giving attention to everything and everyone else besides himself. If he was a stronger, more confident man who had a life outside of the crime solving, perhaps the crime solving would also fall into place.

He hadn't had much luck in that department, and that could only be attributed to the rest of his life falling apart. He had a talent for solving puzzles and latching onto cases that paid off in the end. Something was off the scale here, and he needed to bring it back before he could continue that work in the right way.

He gained back an ounce of confidence with each stroke of his face, then watched the hair hit the floor tile and rush for the drain. When he finished, he set his razor on the soap dish. After the rest of the soap disappeared, he turned off the water with a squeak of the pipes and stepped out into the fogged bathroom.

Just as he left the bathroom, he spotted his phone on the end table, which lit up with a notification. He reluctantly walked over and scanned the screen. It was from the dating app he'd set up earlier.

He had a match.

That was a good feeling. Somebody looked at his photo and his profile, and they wanted to know more about him. Not only that, but it was a somebody that he, too had chosen he was interested in. He was apprehensive about these apps, of course he'd rather meet somebody more organically, however it was rough in this culture to do that.

If he wanted to meet someone, especially as a gay man, he'd have to go to some gay bar or club, or some other event like that. Jonah hated going to those things because it always appeared that they were some kind of meat market. Of course, he was fine with a lonely one night stand here or there, but he was also interested in finding something more than that. Something more substantial, or that would lead to a few more dates if he was going to invest his time and interest in another human being.

He'd set filters on the profile of this dating app so that the guy on the other side knew he wasn't just looking for a hookup. Of course, there was always the possibility of that still happening, but a lesser chance, he'd like to hope. And he wasn't in his college years anymore. He was a grown ass man, with a grown ass job, and he respected himself enough to not subject himself to one night of meaningless comfort.

He looked down at the app. The guy was cute. Definitely his type. He had a resemblance to Mario Lopez. He was a physician of some sort— a bone specialist, also a bonus. He had a real job.

Jonah smiled as he texted the guy and asked if he wanted to meet at a classy club downtown. They could grab a drink and chat, but if it didn't work out, they could easily part ways.

Meeting someone on an app was awkward to begin with, there was no way to avoid that, but at least they were both in the same boat on that one.

When the texts came back that he agreed, something leaped in Jonah's chest, and he realized he hadn't felt that kind of positive anticipation in quite some time. Not even the experience he had when he'd caught onto some big clue in a case. It wasn't the kind of anticipation that sped up his heart and made him feel important, or essential to the work. It was different. Refreshing.

He opened the closet and looked at the array of clothing on the floor to choose from. Jeans, naturally. But what kind of shirt? He should have done laundry. Whatever he chose was going to be wrinkled. Perhaps he could use that as a conversation starter. He chose a v neck, hunter green t-shirt with sleeves that fit snug around his biceps.

He grabbed his phone and wallet, leaving his gun on the nightstand. Work stayed home tonight. Then he looked in his body mirror.

"This is as good as it's gonna get." He liked what he saw reflected back at him. He looked like himself for once. Of course, he could never rid of the scars he bore underneath his clothes from the work that he chose to love, but for one night he could be whoever he wanted to be.

After all, he was a free man with a second chance. Right?

He didn't remember the music being this loud the last time he was here, however long ago that was. It was nearing the evening, so the cocktail hour businessfolk were beginning to clear out, and the evening dates were filtering in. The music was pleasant with a nice beat, and it almost made him feel like he wanted to bob his head to it.

Don't be so rigid. He weaved through the people that clogged up the entryway into the club and made his way up to the bar. He stood behind two woman who were wearing dresses that seemed to be fused to their skin. They turned around, the one girl whipping her hair into his face, and left with their drinks and allowed him the space to lean forward on the bar to grab the attention of the bartender, who was tossing a scoop of ice into a shaker.

"What's your drink?" she asked.

"Uhh, an old fashioned please," he yelled over the loud music.

She nodded and got to work after she handed off a glass to another person and set to fix his drink.

Jonah glanced around, looking for a dark haired, handsome man. The thing with the internet and dating is that people didn't always look like their pictures. And sometimes their height surprised him, or their age. He was hoping this night didn't turn out to be a shit show. He should have looked into the guy before agreeing to meet up. Surely there was more information out there on him. Though the less of a record he could find on someone, the better.

No, Jonah. No work tonight. No investigator mind tonight. He thanked the bartender and tipped her as he picked up his glass and turned to see if there were any open tables. He spotted one several lanes down and bolted for it before it was scooped up.

He hoisted onto the high stool and took a sip of the drink, which tasted fairly weak, of course, because they wanted him to spend more money for a decent buzz. He texted the guy that he was the one sitting at a high top table wearing a hunter green v neck.

"Jonah?"

Wow, that was extremely fast he thought, and then cranked his neck to see that it was not who he'd expected. The voice came from a black man standing behind him, who came around and leaned onto the table.

"Well I didn't expect to see you here!"

"Marcus, hey my man." Jonah stood and threw out his hand, which Marcus took and they bumped shoulders. "What are you doing here?" He took a quick glance around to see if anybody looked like they were reading a text or searching for him.

"Oh you know, just getting out. Socializing. Hoping maybe I'll meet someone who's as lonely as I am. Oh sorry man, didn't mean to get deep."

Jonah forced a small laugh.

"What about you?"

"Oh me? I'm meeting someone here."

"Nice!"

"I didn't realize you were so lonely, you seem to be a ladies man."

Marcus laughed heartily with his white, straight teeth. "Naw man, you saw the shit that happened with me and Raine unfold, and then I was into the new girl in my office, Lilly, but she's all adamant on this not dating coworkers thing. Which I respect. So I've just been solo for a while."

His eyes glazed over. *For once. Just once in my life, can I go through a single night without having to think about that girl, Raine?* "Well, sometimes it's better that way."

"Doesn't sound like it, if you're here to meet someone."

Jonah laughed and looked around, worried his date could show at any moment and possibly hear his conversation. "Well I did the solo thing for a while too, thinking that my work was more important and didn't allow for a relationship. But we're still humans, right? And after a while you're ready to go out again and meet people. Maybe just take some time for yourself and then get out there? Or continue to do your social routine and perhaps it'll find you. Looks like you're already doing that considering you're here right now, yeah?"

"Smart man." Marcus clapped him in the back. "Hey, I'll get out of here so you can enjoy your night. Good to see you and catch up, okay?"

Just then, Jonah had a thought. He was upset that Marcus mentioned Raine before, but then he remembered that perhaps hearing information about her was better for his research. Before he could bite his tongue, the words escaped his lips. "Hey, real fast, sorry to bring this up but I was just curious about this and since I've got you here, how is it working with someone you've had a relationship with?"

"Uhhh, you sure you want to know? I'm going to need another drink for this conversation."

Jonah laughed. "I'm sorry, that was inappropriate of me to ask."

"Naw man, without going into too much detail, it's rough. I've actually had to send her on leave because it's getting more and more difficult to see her every day. Especially since she's been with that one guy. I can't see them together. I'm not over her even though I know I have to be."

"You sent her on leave?"

"Yeah," he nervous laughed. "Told her she was too distracted with everything that had been going on in her life that she needed to take some time off."

Interesting... more time for what? To drive to vacation homes of shady professors that she used to associate with? Just that small amount of information from Marcus was enough. And then he cursed himself. This was supposed to be a workless night, and here he was, always working.

"Jonah?" A soft voice rang out behind him.

"Hey, yeah that's me. You must be Brian?"

"Yeah, did I catch you at a bad time?" The gorgeous man looked from Marcus to Jonah and back again.

"Naw, I was just leaving..." Marcus started.

"He's a friend." Jonah contributed.

Brian smiled, "Sorry, I didn't mean to interrupt."

"Naw, all good. Hey, have a good night Jonah, see you around." Marcus turned and headed back toward the bar.

"I didn't mean to make your friend leave—"

"Naw, don't worry. That was an unexpected visit. Please, have a seat, what's your drink?"

Brian popped up on the chair. "What's in your glass? I'm happy with whatever you're drinking."

"Save our table, I'll go get us some."

"You look just like your photo." Brian smiled.

"I hope that's a good thing?" Jonah laughed.

"It's a very good thing."

Jonah felt his cheeks flush, though he turned his face away and headed for the bar. He was definitely going to need a bit more alcohol in his system before he could loosen up. Especially after the conversation he'd had with Marcus.

It wasn't long before he'd returned to the table, and the drinks and conversation began to flow. He was enjoying his conversation with Brian more than he thought he would, and with the bourbon in his bloodstream, it was easier and easier to say things without the filter. It felt good to let loose, and with each sip of his drink he became more carefree.

"You want to get outta here?" Brian asked, after a few hours of laughing and chatting and drinking at the table.

He did. He did want to get out of here.

"Yeah... but could we go to your place?" he asked.

"What do you live with your mom or something?" Brian asked, laughing.

Jonah liked his sense of humor.

"I knew there'd be a catch to you somewhere."

Ha! Little does he know... "My place is just... messy. Doing some remodeling..." he lied. What he really meant to say was that he had a giant mural on the wall of his family room of a series of crime cases and all of the sensitive details involved. There was no way he could bring anyone back to that apartment. And he did feel guilty for starting their relationship off with a lie, but at this point, with the alcohol in his system, he didn't really care.

He followed Brian outside the club, where others were gathered in groups, waiting on rides, sharing a smoke, or just wanting to get some outside air.

Brian looked down at his phone as it lit up. "They should be pulling up. A black sedan," he relayed.

Jonah looked up and down the road, though it was hard to pinpoint the make of the car in the dark.

"Hey, isn't that your friend?"

His head turned in the direction of Brian's finger, down the lane of cars, where it seemed as though a loud argument had broken out. Two men shouted at each other, one from inside the backseat of the vehicle, one leaned into the car.

Marcus? Jonah thought, squinting his eyes to try and make him out in the dark. What was going on? Should he go see that he was okay? The windows in the car were tinted black, but a bald man leaned out of the window a moment. It appeared as though Marcus knew the person, judging by his body language. Surely alcohol was involved. Jonah had a bit of his own inside him as well and wasn't completely clearheaded. The last thing he wanted was to get in a fight when he was having a nice time with Brian, and he wasn't supposed to be working. He promised himself that he'd shut off his PI mind for just one night and enjoy the company of someone new that he could possibly make a connection with. He looked back at Brian, who had located the ride-share. "He'll be okay."

"You sure? I don't mind if you want to check it out."

But it did sound like Brian minded. And Jonah was really liking how their night was going.. He hopped into the back of the car with Brian and secured his seat belt, pulling the door closed. "I'm sure." He smiled and leaned his head back on the seat.

Even though he wasn't working tonight, he wouldn't forget what he saw as he left the club. Marcus, in an altercation with somebody in a high profile, tinted vehicle, in which he gave in, and took off in the car with them.

THE DOMINO EFFECT

FOURTEEN

Raine Walsh

R aine threw her arms around Chloe and hugged her close, her face smashing into her sister's blonde hair. She backed up and held her by the shoulders.

"Can't you come with me? Come on..."

She bent down and picked up her sister's suitcase, moving it along in the long line to check it into the airline. "Geeze, what do you have in here? Bricks?" she laughed, but Chloe did not return the sentiment.

"I'm serious. You need to get away from all this."

"I can't. I can't run away from my problems. And as we saw, I also can't protect you here. As long as I have things going on here, you'll always be in danger because your association with me. You're my weakness. I can't have you hurt."

"Well I can't have you hurt either!"

"I'll be fine, okay? And after it's all over, maybe we can take a girl's trip or something. And get far away from here. Maybe Europe?"

"After what is all over? How do you know when whatever it is that's happening is going to be over?"

She had seriously considered skipping town. What would happen if she'd left, with Jensen keeping a close eye on her to see if she proved herself worthy to work with him? The threat would never go away. Not until he was dead.

"Next in line!" The airline attendant called them up to the desk, and Chloe shuffled for her ticket and license.

Raine hoisted the suitcase onto the weighing belt for her. They finished the transaction and walked away, following the signs to the TSA line.

"I'm going to miss you," she said to her sister, who had gone quiet, probably knowing that she couldn't convince Raine. "Plus, I know I grew up in Ohio with you and the family, but my life is here now. Viona is here. My home is here. Arie is here. My work..." Her voice trembled on that last one. "I can't just run away from that. You haven't been here long enough to plant those roots yet, and things have happened to you," she avoided flat out saying her boyfriend was murdered. "You need to have some time away from those memories."

"I know, I know. I'm just gonna miss you too. And it's not fair, all of this."

Raine looked down at her feet, her eyelashes fluttering over her lids. "No, it's not," she whispered. She roped her arms around Chloe one last time before it was time for her sister to cross the airport security checkpoint. Raine watched her until she went all the way through, then she turned around and headed back out.

She texted Arie, and then headed back to her apartment to return the car.

That night, Raine stood in the shower and allowed the water to flow over her until it wasn't warm anymore, and Arie had to knock on the door to check on her. The entire evening consisted of drowning in her own thoughts.

It was unspoken that they'd both be more comfortable with Arie spending the night. They lay awake in the bed together. He heaved a long sigh.

"What?" she asked.

"Are you gonna tell me what happened?" he asked.

Her lips pursed. She wasn't sure. She'd had the entire drive home to think about what to say to him. It would have been easy to tell him the absolute and complete truth. If she was going to tell any person, it would be him. But she also didn't *want* him to know the truth.

The professor would like that.

And he would find out.

She rolled over in the bed, faced away from Arie. Viona reluctantly took the couch that night since *somebody* was in her usual spot. In the dark apartment, Raine's eyes dilated and she stared at the wall until she heard the deep breathing of Arie behind her. He was asleep. She lay, listening to the vents in the walls of her studio apartment, thinking about an urge that crossed her mind.

Raine Walsh was done being the victim.

She ran over in her head once again all the times she had been victim, trying to pull out some piece of the puzzle that she was missing. Something that could help her prove her loyalty to the work.

The Warden. What had happened in his life that made him act the way he did? Why would this man want to recreate a prison in the penthouse of his skyscraper? He had money. Couldn't he do what he wanted with that? *Well, I guess he did...* Was he trying to recreate a psychological study that went so awfully wrong because he could do it better? What was he trying to show of humanity? Resilience? Purpose?

She was the victim in that case, but she'd never thought about Allen's perspective. What a sad life that was... Had he been bullied himself? Had he had such suggestibility that he would perform horrific experiments on other people to prove a point that was lost on most everyone?

But there wasn't just him. There was Vinnie. Raine had known Vinnie on another level. She was his and his wife's therapist. Vinnie had a beautiful wife and new baby. He had a life. What was so terrible about his life that he had to kill? This was where her experience in psychology should come into play, but she still didn't quite understand his urges, or the multiple personalities she had seen in him during her time knowing him. There was something deeper she was missing.

What about this last case, the most perplexing one of all? The experiment that took place in the basement of Professor Jensen's while he was gone. The one concerning the carbon copy of another one of her clients, Tanner.

It seemed as though all of these people were acting, not on their own accord, but acting from some force that was possessing them to take the actions they did. What happened in their lives that led them to that point?

No parent thinks they're raising a serial killer. Were those tendencies nurture or nature?

If *they* were capable...*was she capable? Of murder?* She remembered back to her time in the prison when she'd unleashed on that guard that was trying to stop her from escaping. She beat the shit out of him. At the time she felt like she had to, to get to her end goal, and he was stopping her. But after impairing him, she continued to unleash her fury. *Was that necessary? Where did that spark of violence from within her come from? Was there more?*

And why was she suddenly having these thoughts? Had these thoughts always been buried deep within her subconscious and she'd covered them up this entire time?

Raine kicked off her slip-on shoes and held them by the heels as she walked into the soft, cushioned sand. Her feet sank into the grains, and she looked at her every step as she walked toward the water. The beach was vacant. Generally, there weren't any swimmers on the Bay Area beaches, except for a few crazy tourists that didn't realize the water was exceptionally cold. To them, a beach was a beach.

She was like that when she first moved to the West Coast. When you're from the east or Midwest part of the United States, and grew up there with piles of snow and mild summers, any beach is a beach to you.

The beach was a welcomed detour back from the airport, and always a place of healing for her that she took for granted living so close by. And right now she needed clarity. Since she'd been told not to come in to work, now was the perfect moment to get some quiet time to herself.

When she got close enough to the water but still in dry sand, she plopped down on the ground and set her shoes next to her. She sat cross legged and breathed deep from within, listening to the waves come onto the shore and retreat. It wasn't long before her breaths matched the pattern of the waves, as though the biggest body on Earth were breathing right there alongside her, inviting her to get lost in its cadence of healing. She closed her eyes and let it consume her body and soul before allowing thought back into her mind.

How do I go about researching what Jensen wants? She continued to keep her eyes closed as she channeled this thought. She recalled the entire time she'd known him, from the beginning, in the early psychology classes, where she dreaded going because he was a pompous ass. He'd give lectures as though nobody were in the room listening. He didn't allow questions, and if you missed something, good luck on the next exam.

She'd record his lectures on her phone to listen to later, but sometimes he was speaking so fast and slurred that it sounded like gibberish. How had she always found ways to please him before to pass his class?

Resistance. She'd always played against the grain. When most of the time she'd keep her mouth shut and let it be because perhaps that's the way it was supposed to be for her, she'd always speak up in his case. Or distance herself. Or refuse to do the extra bit he'd always pack on.

It got her thinking about more recent events. How did she know it was the professor who took Chloe? And how did she get out of that mess? The reason Jensen took Chloe, apart from his henchman thinking it was Raine to begin with, was because he knew that it was an easy way to get to Raine. He knew that he needed some kind of bait, because Raine wanted nothing to do with him.

Bingo.

That was it. He was always attracted to her like a magnet because she resisted. He wanted her to join the elite club he sponsored and she said no.

She didn't want to associate with him when she didn't have to. So why now, after everything, did she want to work alongside him as a colleague? And she knew nothing about this secret work—except that it warranted murder when someone got in the way.

And if in the past she'd gotten his attention by doing nothing and staying far away, then maybe that's what she needed to do now? It seemed easy enough. But Raine was a thinker, and it was hard to shut that off.

She brought her attention back to her surroundings and opened her eyes, leaning back in the soft sand. She thought about how she wasn't at work right now. Why did Marcus want her to take a leave? What were his intentions exactly? She couldn't help but think of it again. Did he really care for her well-being and notice that she'd been having a tough time lately? Or was there some reason he wanted her away from the office?

They hadn't had a great relationship as of late. She hadn't even thought about how it must have made him feel to see her all the time. Surely, he'd moved on by now. She was becoming closer to Lilly, and told Lilly if she wanted to be with Marcus, good luck, in a joking way—and Lilly informed her that she did not date coworkers, and that Marcus was barking up the wrong tree. That made Raine laugh, and made her appreciate Lilly more, but she sort of felt bad for Marcus.

Until she wondered about his intentions again, and how weird he'd been acting lately, and all the questionable things in their history that made her second-guess him. She just wasn't sure whether or not she could trust him.

It was as though the universe could hear her thinking about that, because just then, her phone began to vibrate in her pocket. She thought about letting it go to voicemail and continuing to enjoy nature, but it could be a number of important phone calls.

It could be Chloe saying she'd landed. It could be Arie saying he was back at her apartment from work, or asking if she wanted to meet for lunch. It could be Heely... though their last conversation went terribly, so it wasn't likely.

But no. It was none of them.

It was her office. Maybe it was Sylvie? She never really got to tell her goodbye before her leave.

"Hello?" she asked, worried that the sound of the ocean would interfere with the reception.

"Raine? Can you talk?" It was Lilly. Her voice sounded urgent.

"Sure, what's going on?"

"Uhh, I have an incident here... with a client. I'm not entirely sure what to do. They've locked themselves in my office. I've called the police, but I'm afraid anything official will frighten them even more. It's one of your clients that I've taken on and I just don't know their file well enough to help. I didn't know if you were close or... or if you were willing." Her voice was panic-stricken and frantic, something Raine had never heard before.

"Is Marcus there? Can he help until I get there?" she asked. She was also worried that he'd be mad if she came in and was slightly curious whether or not he knew that Lilly was calling her for help.

"No," she said quickly. "He uhhh, he actually hasn't been in the office in several days. I thought you knew."

"What? Why?" Right after she asked, she knew there wasn't time over the phone to get the details.

"I thought he was sick at first but then his phone goes straight to voicemail, so I don't know." She sounded irritated.

"Lilly, I'm sorry. I'll be there soon. Just... keep them talking, okay? Help the client with some breathing exercises. You can tell them I'm on the way."

"Thank you."

Raine hung up the phone and crawled to her feet. Then, she rushed back toward the parking lot.

The sand beneath her feet made it a challenge to do anything quickly. It felt like she was sinking with every step, sinking deeper into oblivion.

SIXTEEN

Raine Walsh

Raine stepped off the streetcar and bolted through a crowd. It was times like these that she wished she owned her own vehicle. It was nice to be able to borrow Arie's neighbor's car, but she should probably invest in one herself—her last car had been burned in the car fire when she was taken. Of course, she didn't really like driving. It seemed dangerous, and she would much rather be more economically and environmentally conscious of her carbon footprint in this busy city. San Francisco was no stranger to public transportation, and the city mostly offered her everything she needed.

But when it came to getting somewhere quickly, it became more of a nuisance than anything. The clinic wasn't far enough away to warrant a ride share, but it didn't seem close enough to wait for all the stops either.

But she was here now and she raced for the office door. She felt off, as tore into the practice. There were a few wor-ried faces in the waiting room who looked at her and back toward the commotion happening down the hall.

"Oh, Raine..." Sylvie rushed down the hall, motioning for her to follow.

Raine had now finally recognized it as her office, as opposed to thinking of it as Troy's.

She assessed the situation—Lilly was up against the door, and there was yelling and crashing from inside the office.

"Who is it?"

"Anastasia Cruz," Lilly said, her face frantic. She was stressed beyond what she could handle.

Anya. Raine was familiar with her, although it'd been a while since she'd seen her. "Anya?" she called, placing her hands on the door. "Will you let me in?"

"NO!"

"Has somebody called the police? Her parents also need to be called. She's not a minor, she's eighteen, but they likely don't know she's here."

"Police are coming, we told them to come quietly, so they don't spook her." Lilly whispered into her ear.

Raine nodded, "Good idea. She's probably off her meds, so we need to handle this according to protocol. But she's also a human being, so she needs compassion."

"She's probably destroyed my office by now." Lilly grumbled under her breath so that Raine just barely heard it. She understood though. Feeling complete lack of control over your personal possessions inside would be overwhelming.

"Keys?"

"Inside. Don't you think we've already thought of that?" Lilly snapped.

Raine allowed her. Lilly was stressed and had had to handle this situation a lot longer than she had. "Anya, it's Dr. Walsh. I'd love to see you. It's been such a long time."

There was a moment of silence. Raine tucked her chin and looked back at the two women hopeful it worked.

"Nobody else?"

"Just me. I'd love to talk with you." There was another moment of silence and Raine motioned for the other two to back up.

The lock on the door clicked and the door cracked open. Raine slipped inside and shut the door behind her.

Anastasia had backed up to the desk. Papers and books and things of Lilly's were strewn across the floor. She was wearing dark jeans and a black hoodie, with the hood up. Her eyes were bugged out. "You left."

Raine allowed the words to sink in. One of her biggest fears when she started to fade from the practice because of her own issues was that she would be leaving her clients. She was worried she'd abandoned them. But also knew that she had to do what was best for her, or she wouldn't have been able to help anybody.

"You left just like you did before."

"I know, Anya. I needed some time off. I didn't want to, and Dr. Everstein is a great person to talk to. Did you give her a chance?"

"She said I need medication."

Raine tilted her head to Anastasia. "You and I both know that that is not wrong. Don't you feel better when you have it?"

"It makes me numb."

"If that's the case, then we need to change it. That one is not right for your body."

"Why do I have to take it?" She crossed her arms over her chest, acting like an adolescent. Of course, she was only eighteen, but she was not showing any signs of maturity.

"We both know the answer to that one as well. Why does anyone take any kind of medicine? To help them feel better. Do your parents know you're here?"

She shook her head, her eyes growing dark. "They don't care."

"Now you know that's not true, Anya. They love you very much and are probably so worried about where you are right now. I'm happy you came here, because you know this is a safe place."

"But you weren't here."

"Well I can't be here all the time, right? I have things I need to get done in my life as well."

Anastasia nodded.

"Why did you get so upset?" Raine motioned to the mess around the office.

"I didn't know what to do." She looked down. "I feel bad. I felt trapped and this lady was just telling me things when she didn't even know me. Like I was just some customer and not a person who has feelings. I was just a file in her hands."

"Like I said, Dr. Everstein was trying to catch up to the point where we were by going through your file. I can assure you that she's only here to help you and she wants to help you. We're not like the other doctors you've had experiences with, okay? We want to help you."

Anya looked down.

Why did this girl want *Raine* to help her, out of everyone? Because she trusted her. Because Raine built a relationship with her, even if they hadn't seen each other in a long time. She carried that experience with her and it allowed her to live her life normally, without interruption.

"Why did you feel the need to come here?" Raine asked. She was trying to gauge the situation without triggering anything.

"I got in a fight with my Mom."

"Do you want to talk about it?"

"She thinks I don't do anything all day long and she makes me do chores."

"Well, you do live in her house, Anya. She's just being a mom and I'm sure she's worried about you right now. I've met your mom. I know I don't know her like you do, but her intentions are to help you be self-sufficient."

Anastasia looked down again.

"What do you think about us getting out of this room?" she asked.

The distraught teen nodded.

"Do you want to help me clean up this mess for Dr. Everstein? It's not fair if she has to do it by herself."

She nodded again and began to pick up papers.

"I'm just going to let everyone know that it's okay, and that we'll be out in just a little bit, okay?"

"Everyone?"

"We don't want to scare you—"

"I knew it! I trusted you, Dr. Walsh!" She yelled, throwing the papers to the floor again.

"Anya, listen. We didn't know what you were doing in here. If you were hurting yourself or planned to hurt others. So authorities were called. But you've calmed down now— right? So, none of that is necessary anymore. You've seen this before, we're all here working together to make sure you're safe and to help you." When she saw that Anastasia had acknowledged what she said and began to breathe normally again, she gently grabbed the handle of the door and cracked it open, sticking her head out.

Lilly and Sylvie looked at her with wide, hopeful, inquiring eyes.

"We're just going to clean up the office and we'll be right out."

"Oh, that's not necessary." Lilly whispered back as though it was no big deal.

"She needs this," Raine finalized.

Sylvie interjected, "Police are in the waiting room, what should I tell them?"

"She's willing to speak with them, but she's not in trouble and she's not going to cause any more trouble, okay?"

Sylvie nodded and shuffled toward the waiting room.

"Thank you," Lilly mouthed to Raine.

She let out a small smile, and then slipped back inside the office.

After Raine helped her client finish picking up Lilly's office and then escorted her out to speak to the police and get a ride home, she slinked back into the office to see if Lilly was still in there.

Leaning in the doorframe, she asked, "So where did you say Marcus was?"

Lilly turned around, her face white. "I don't know. He hasn't been here for several days."

"That's not like him. He told me not to come in. I was actually kind of ego bruised by that but felt like he was probably right. And now he's not even showing up for work? I can't imagine the workload you've taken on, Lilly."

She shrugged. "It's the job, right?"

"I mean, not really. You shouldn't be taking on all these clients. Look at what happened today. And I'm not—" She tried to finish what she was saying without allowing Lilly to interrupt. "I'm not saying you're incapable of doing this because you fully are. I'm just saying you don't deserve that stress. Our profession is all about building rapport."

Lilly nodded. "I know what you meant. Thank you for coming and helping out. I really wanted to defuse that situation instead of scaring her even more, or escalating to where she might hurt herself, and you helped with that. You were great with her."

"Anytime... seriously. Do you guys need any more help today?"

"Naw, we're okay now. I only have my own clients the rest of the day. Sylvie's been rescheduling all of Marcus's clients until we hear something from him."

Raine nodded. "Take it easy, all right? Feel free to use my yoga studio if you'd like."

She smiled and nodded in return.

Raine turned from the office and headed back to the public transportation to take the train back to her apartment. She was going to go check on Viona, and then head to Arie's place for dinner. He'd offered to make her dinner since she'd been so stressed lately, and now that her sister was back home in Ohio, things had been quiet. She was looking forward to a nice, calm night with Arie, where she could perhaps put everything to the side and just spend time with him.

It did cross her mind that she had been concerned where Marcus was. It wasn't like him to just not show up for work. However, she currently did not trust him at all. Though it was none of her business. There was the possibility that he was in danger. But why would Marcus be targeted?

And by who?

SIXTEEN

Raine Walsh

Arie insisted that she'd stay the night after they finished dinner, but she wanted to get back to Viona. That, and she wasn't sure they were in the point in their relationship for her to stay over, even if they had done it before, and even if they really would be just sleeping. She was so happy with how things were going, and it was as if she couldn't get enough of spending time with him doing normal things.

As she headed home, something else crossed her mind. If she was going to be engaging in a project with Professor Jensen that was revolutionary and completely confidential, she might need to distance herself from Arie—which was the very last thing in the world that she wanted to do. Perhaps Jensen would view Arie as a distraction or a threat to the research, like he did Alex. She had to protect him. She'd done a terrible job of protecting her sister, and she wasn't sure how much control she'd have over protecting the other people she loved when it came to engaging in this dangerous game with Jensen.

Then she thought about herself. The fact that she helped Lilly with her client today really boosted her confidence in her ability, willingness, and desire to help people and see that through. If that was the case, was she really capable of horrible things? Could she really begin to compare herself to the serial killers and bad people she'd helped put away in the past years? Sure, there were similarities as Jensen had pointed out. The rest of them were students that went to the same university as her. But what were the odds that they were all living within the same vicinity? That wasn't a good enough comparison. It was when she analyzed their psyche that she discovered more possible similarities, which was something she didn't tend to enjoy doing quite often, because it gave her an uneasy feeling.

It was a short walk from the bus station to her apartment, and the night was young. She was so close to her apartment that she thought she might pass it and go to a small coffeehouse down the street to grab a cup of tea before going home. If she could grab an herbal tea without having to make it herself, it would help her to relax and fall asleep better.

She floated toward the cafe and into the shop. The employees were diligently working, sweeping the floors and working down their cleaning task lists. The place was nearly empty. As she walked inside and the bell jingled on the door behind her, she looked around. "Are you guys closed?" she asked the young barista sweeping the floor.

"Oh no, you're good. We're just catching up on some cleaning," he responded and then went back to his work.

She smiled and approached the counter. "I'll just have a small chamomile tea, please."

"That's an easy one!" The barista behind the counter said as they grabbed a cup and prepped the loose-leaf tea in the tea sac.

"Usually I'd bring my reusable cup but I haven't been home yet."

"Oh no worries, there's always next time, right!"

Raine smiled. They were really friendly, even though she knew they were probably trying to close so they could go home. She was grateful they let her get her drink. As the water hit the tea sac while the barista prepared it, Raine smelled the sweet, soothing scent of the chamomile flowers. So calming. So nice.

She got the cup from the barista, paid for it, and then went on her way. She left the shop with another ring of the bell and headed back down the street toward her apartment. Naturally the tea had to steep, so she'd need to wait for it to cool down a bit before she could sip it, but at least she didn't have to make it at home now.

The sky had gotten darker and a whistle blew past her in the wind. She looked back and forth and crossed the street, nearing her apartment. She was wearing a light wind jacket and she pulled the collar up around her neck with her free arm. It seemed as though nobody was around. That was, until she felt like there were eyes on her.

C'mon, Raine... you're NOT always being followed, she told herself to build her confidence as she quickened her pace. It was then that she heard the car engine. It was quiet, but it was consistent. Not the sound of a passing car. This one was driving slow, slower than she was walking. She dared and looked back over her shoulder. The car was dark, no headlights, which was also unusual, and the moment she saw it she snapped her head back.

They *were* following her.

She was almost to her apartment. She dropped the tea, spilling it all over the palm of her hand as she took off at a run. The adrenaline stopped her from feeling the burn, and the moment she heard the car door, she ran faster. She frantically looked around for someone, anyone to be around, but the street was getting darker, and the number of pedestrians was small, just like in the coffeehouse.

"Help!" she screamed, as the person chasing her gained on her. Her voice came out as a screech, as though she were in a dream and could not control her vocal chords. As though she was running in quicksand, and her senses were beginning to fade, her line of sight, the capacity of her lungs.

Without getting the chance to look, she felt pressure on her lower back and legs, and it sent her flying to the ground. She tried to put her hands out to catch the fall, and she shut her eyes as the pavement met her body.

She wiggled and thrashed, but the person was just too strong. The car pulled up next to them and the door flung open. She looked over at the wheels of the car on the pavement. Flashbacks of her first year in college came flooding back to her. The man with the trench coat. How he was so much stronger than her. The person behind her towered her in strength, and forced it upon her. She kicked, tried to bite, and tried to scream. But nothing seemed to be good enough. Last time she was lucky enough that someone on the street recognized her, that football player from her psychology class. But this time, she was not so lucky.

The man lifted her like it was nothing. She tried several different self-defense moves she'd learned, but everything seemed to be blocked. This person was also very well trained in self-defense. As he dragged her around to the back of the car, she tried everything she could to get away.

She heard the sound of the trunk pop open, and her body tossed like a rag doll. As she rolled over the carpeted inside, she tried to get up when the door was slammed shut and knocked her back down.

She kicked and smashed her hands into the inside of the trunk of the car, but it was no use. The engine revved up, louder than her cries, and she rolled over again from the momentum of the car jerking forward into the night.

SEVENTEEN

Raine Walsh

S he'd heard about being locked in the trunk of a car. She'd already exhausted herself from pounding and should probably conserve her energy for when the door opened again.

It was small, dark, and smelled of musty tobacco. The scent almost made her choke, and her burned hand was beginning to sting.

Her lungs began to tighten as well, and she needed to calm down if she was planning on not having a panic attack in this enclosed space. She closed her eyes and focused on her breathing. She didn't take deep breaths, because she didn't want to take all of the oxygen out of the small space and make herself pass out, but she regulated her breathing. The same amount of breath taken in was the same amount of breath let out. Her hand throbbed from the boiling tea water spilling down the outside of her hand on the thin skin there.

It was a feeling she'd never felt before, not one of anxiety or fear, but one of anger. She was going home to have a nice relaxing night with her sleepy tea and her dog after a wonderful night with her new boyfriend.

The person that took her was a jerk! And she was just downright upset about it. When the car took a turn, she rolled in the trunk, trying to hold on. At least they hadn't knocked her out, like her experience in the past. She wondered where they were going and was mad that she hadn't been paying attention. She'd been too flustered to see which direction they'd gone from the street in front of her apartment.

She tried to recall a television show she'd seen about being locked in trunks. She felt around for any kind of latch she could pop open. The door seemed smooth, with no way of unlatching from the inside.

Then it hit her.

Her phone! How had she not thought about that lifeline before? She dug into her back pockets and her stomach sank. It wasn't there. She must have lost it on the pavement during the scuffle. That was another bruise to her hope.

She wallowed in that loss for a minute before she began to think of what moves to pull when the trunk opened, which she hoped was soon as she rolled again at a turn.

Who will miss me? She tried to think who would notice that she was gone or that something was wrong. She didn't have any particular dates planned. Arie would know something was wrong when he tried to call and she didn't answer, but who knew how long that would be? He might be thinking that he needed to give her space after their nice evening together in order to not smother her. He knew she wanted to take their relationship slowly.

Truth is, she wanted to just go with the flow and take it as it came. And it seemed like she wanted to be with him constantly. She hated that she hadn't expressed that with him more fully. But then there was also the thought that she wanted to keep distance from him, so that Jensen didn't see him as a threat or distraction to their work.

Jensen. Was he at the bottom of this kidnapping? Why would he do this so soon? It didn't make sense.

The truth of the matter was, she didn't have anyone that would be looking or expecting her anytime soon.

There was one last thing she could try. She was wearing slip-on shoes, so she didn't have much leverage, but she pulled down the felt fabric inside the trunk toward the car. She felt around the metal for the back of the tail lights. Then she maneuvered her body in the trunk to have her feet resting on the back light.

"Here goes nothing..." she breathed and then shoved her foot into the back of the tail light. A pain shot up her shin, as she'd hit it in just the perfect spot to feel pain, and then she kicked at it again. She only had a few moments to try this before the person up front, or people, since there must have been a driver and a grabber, heard her making commotion back there. She kicked at it again, ignoring the pain. She was able to pop out the light, which hung out the back of the car.

A gust of cool wind flew into the trunk, and she quickly turned her body around as best as she could in the tight space. First of all, the air felt amazing. She breathed it in as much as she could, choking on the wind that flooded inside. Then she tried to look out, but the way she was tucked in the trunk made it difficult to see anything. It was very dark outside now, and the passing lights indicated they were still in the city.

She tried to poke her hand out, then waved it around outside the vehicle. The hope was that a car driving behind that car would see her and notify the police.

She waved her hand, the one that was burned because it felt good to be out in the cold, until it began to cramp. Nobody was seeing her. Her last ditch effort, and the little light of hope of catching someone's attention was diminishing with every passing minute. She pulled her hand back in and lay on her side, waiting, just waiting for what was to come next.

It wasn't long before the car came to a stop. Voices argued outside the car, but she couldn't quite make out what they were saying. It was only a matter of time before they came to let her out.

Next came a jingling of keys and she prepared herself to fight when the time came. But when the trunk opened, she saw the barrel of a gun pointed directly between her eyes.

"Don't even think about it," a man said. His voice was deep, as she imagined a troll's voice would sound. She saw that he was white, and bald, and she tried to pinpoint as many features as she could while she got one good look at him.

"I'll cooperate," she said quickly.

He almost laughed. "Bet your ass you will." He huffed. "Turn around."

She did as he demanded. She wasn't sure what was at the end of this, but she'd gotten out of it before, and she was almost positive that this situation was related to recent events. There was no way this was an isolated incident. That just didn't happen to people, unless she was terribly, terribly unlucky— which was possible.

She turned on her knees in the trunk with her hands up as though she'd surrendered. He threw a black scarf in front on her face and pulled it up onto her eyes, blindfolding her.

"Is this necessary? I told you I'd do as you said."

He didn't respond, but tied it tightly on her head, almost too tightly as she felt the knot of the fabric on the back of her head. At least this was better than being knocked out, she hoped, because she'd been there as well, and not having complete and utter control of her body was probably something she feared more than death.

Next, Raine twitched as the man grabbed her chin. At first, she naturally tried to resist in protest, but then she relaxed when she realized she needed to prove her cooperation.

She opened her mouth to tell him that this wasn't necessary, when a large wad of something, a musty tasting fabric, was shoved into her mouth.

She gagged, choking on the fabric, though it muffled her voice. Then the tape came. A layer of sticky, most likely duct tape secured the scarf inside her mouth. She choked on it again before she realized that she was better off breathing in and out through her nostrils, as it was the only way.

The choking brought a moistness to her eyes underneath the blindfold as she was ushered out of the trunk, completely and totally impaired. Her arms were bound behind her back by some sort of plastic zip tie, that was pulled too tightly on her wrist, cutting into her skin.

As he shoved her forward to walk, she had the sinking feeling of not knowing what was in front of her. It felt like when you are walking down the stairs in the dark and you think there is still one more stair at the bottom, only there isn't. With every step forward into the unknown, she grew this sinking feeling more and more.

They went up a short flight of stairs, then through a door. Next came another set of less even, mustier smelling stairs.

Once at the bottom, she was shoved to sit, her legs tied to each leg, and her wrists were fastened to the arms of the chair.

"He'll be down here for you shortly."

She felt the man's hot breath on her ear and she pulled her head away as best she could. And then she heard his footsteps getting farther and farther away, up the stairs with an echo in each hop. Then the creak of a door as it shut.

EIGHTEEN

Raine Walsh

She sat there in complete and utter silence. The wad of fabric in her mouth had been fully drenched from her saliva, and it was drying out her throat. She shifted in the chair, more uncomfortable than she could remember being in a long while.

Her attitude was different from the last time something like this had happened to her. And that was just it. She realized that she'd been through enough that she didn't feel like what was ahead of her could top that. Though she also had a feeling that perhaps she was wrong about that.

Completely wrong.

The door creaked open. Raine's adrenaline kicked into high gear. She'd been sitting down there long enough to build up in her mind what the other guy, the bald guy was getting her ready for. Or who he was getting her ready for. And as she heard the footsteps on the stairs, slowly coming down, she wanted to shout and scream, but she couldn't with the tape over her lips.

The person stepped right in front of her. She couldn't tell if it was light or dark because of the blindfold, though she felt the presence of someone directly in front of her chair.

She flinched when they gripped the side of her face and tugged at the tape. She winced as the tape was slowly pulled from her mouth. She felt it was a friendly gesture, for some reason, but the ginger movement was almost worse. Like ripping off a band-aid. The adhesive was so strong that she felt like the thin, soft skin was being ripped off her lips. After the tape was removed, she pushed the fabric out her mouth with her tongue and took in heaps of breaths.

It didn't take long to realize it wasn't a breath of fresh air. It was musty, even worse and more suffocating than the trunk. The air was wet and dated. She couldn't find any words in her itchy, scratchy throat. Not even a scream.

Next, the person reached up behind her head and began to untie the blindfold. They gently grazed her neck with the tips of their fingers, and she flinched and shrugged her shoulders in disgust, a natural reaction.

She felt a chill across her shoulders, that grazed all the way down her spine, and she began to shake intermittently. Perhaps this could be worse than she was imagining it. Perhaps this person wanted to take advantage of her.

She waited to see who her captor was, and where she had been take to. The blindfold fell from her eyes onto her lap, though she couldn't touch it or grab it because she was still tied to the chair. It took several moments for her eyes to adjust to the light. It was dim, and she looked all around in the cellar. It was an old, dilapidated basement. Low lit, but enough to cast shadows on the stone. She looked up to see the foundation of the house above her, tree trunks used as beams. This was an old, old house. This basement was even older, which explained the musty smell and damp air.

She looked over to the left and felt the presence of her captor. The shadows on the wall indicated that he was standing directly behind her. She tried to find out the appropriate words to say, that would not make this person angry or lash out at her. It was always getting into the psychology of the other person, to say what they are wanting to hear, to get out of the situation. It was never about her in these situations that she found herself in time and time again.

"What do you want with me?" she asked, her voice scratchy and unused and tired.

The person behind her laughed. Of all things... *he laughed.*

She pursed her lips, infuriated. This was no laughing matter to her, and she began to think of who this person could be. Someone who laughed during an inappropriate situation, a psychopath that laughed when they should cry, or laugh when they are hurt but don't understand those social cues. Or, she could be giving him the benefit of the doubt in that situation. This person could just be an asshole, laughing at her expense. Either way, she was sick and tired of playing games and just wanted to get it over with.

She sighed.

Then she heard the footsteps walking around her chair. She squinted and turned her head. The man stood in silhouette, his shadow against the light coming from the staircase.

When he came into view, she nearly peed herself, her stomach flipping as though she'd just been thrown off an upside-down rollercoaster.

"You," she grumbled, shaking, tear stricken, confused, angry, and every overwhelming emotion as it took over her entire aching body and consumed her.

"Yes, me." Marcus replied, his body outlined by the dim hanging lightbulb behind him in the cold, dark, musty basement.

THE DOMINO EFFECT

NINETEEN

Raine Walsh

What frightened her the most, was that when she saw him for the first time as he came into view, she was *not* comforted by his presence. And whether her accusations were correct or not, she somehow ended up here.

Not only had he snatched her on the street outside of her apartment, using this bald guy as an accomplice, she couldn't handle the fact that he'd done it in such violent, heartless manner, as though he never cared for her at all.

"I—I don't know what to say," she croaked.

"Well that's a first," he mocked, laughing again.

"Do you think this is funny?" she whispered, looking away from his gaze. She'd never forgive him for this.

He crossed his arms over his chest.

"What are we doing here, Marcus? What do you want from me?" she asked. Even just forming his name on her tongue gave her a bitter taste. She thought about all the years they'd been close, starting back in college. They were best friends. They started a practice together. They'd been in and out of being lovers. They'd lived together. He'd made her feel safe and protected from the outside world.

And then there was the other end of it as well. He'd made her feel vulnerable. He'd made her feel bad for the decisions she'd made. She lost trust in him after she'd found his belongings that triggered her trauma—like the coffee mug in his apartment that had been the same as the Warden's. Or when he'd gone behind her back and hired Lilly, even though Lilly was brought into the crossfire without knowing.

She didn't understand what the end game was with Marcus, and she wasn't sure whether or not she should have an attitude with him and show him how she really felt, or if she should continue to comply, which had been her original plan for any other captor. Knowing it was him who had her tied to that chair, changed everything.

She tugged at her restraints and scanned the stone walls around them. "Where are we?" she asked, assessing the basement again. She'd never been to this place before, and in that exact moment, she remembered Marcus had been missing from the office for several days.

Her arms and legs itched with anxiety. The light, the mood in the cellar made her antsy.

He stood there and watched her in the chair with amusement, as though he was allowing her to talk herself into the ground. "You're sitting in the same chair, that I sat in only just a few days ago."

It was like a riddle and it hurt her brain to think about what he meant.

"You'd gone missing," she whispered, keeping her quivering eyes locked on his. She couldn't believe she'd loved him at one point, and even in this moment of despair, it hurt her heart to think he could do anything to harm her, after having given him her whole heart at one point.

Do people change? Or were they always innately the way they are? What possesses them, him, to do such things if his personality never showed otherwise? Was it nature that pushed him to do this, or is it nurture and environment? Did I push him to turn into this?

No. She would not blame herself for this. This was all Marcus's decision. "Lilly called me and told me you'd gone missing from the office, they couldn't get a hold of you," she said.

He nodded. "I was taken. Just like you were. Snatched from my apartment. Thrown into a car. Brought to this place and strapped to that chair. I told... I told him to be gentle with you, but that you can also be mouthy sometimes... hence the uhhh, gag and tape."

She narrowed her eyes. She wanted to punch him so hard right now. The moment she got out of these bonds. "Yet now you stand on that side."

He nodded.

"I just want to know, before anything else—"

"You can never just listen."

"Please, just please let me ask this one thing and then I'll be quiet and let you do what you have to." She wasn't entirely sure *that* was true, but she had to say what she had to in the moment.

He continued to stand there with his arms crossed.

"Were you involved the whole time? With everything that happened to me?" She wasn't sure if he knew what she was talking about, but if he was involved, he'd know.

She thought she caught a glimmer of emotion in his eye as he looked away from her toward the corner of the room. It was as though he knew more to the story than he'd ever let on, as though he was afraid that if he shared anything with her, he'd be breaking down his wall of being the tough guy. "Define 'the beginning'."

Her neck grew hot. "Prison?"

"No."

"How did we end up here?" she asked. She noticed he was thinking about it again. Perhaps this was her best bet.

"C'mon, Marcus. You don't have to treat me this way. You don't have to keep me tied to this chair. Which, by the way the ties around my wrists are really hurting me... cutting into my skin."

"There's something I have to tell you."

The hairs on her arms pricked again.

"I've been working for someone that you would have never approved of. If you knew, you'd never speak to me again."

"O....kay..." she offered, trying to hurry him forward. She definitely had plenty of reasons now for not ever speaking to him again. "Marcus, I think we're beyond that at this point." She moved her eyes around to indicate where they were at the moment. "Who?"

"Professor Jensen."

She choked.

"I'd been working with him since before you found out about your sister's boyfriend assisting him, and when I saw how angry you were that night, I sort of just hid it."

"'Sort of'? Seriously?" She wondered what he meant by the fact that he'd been working for Jensen, and what that entailed. She wondered if the conversation she'd had with Jensen back at his vacation home was even truthful, or real, and she wondered once again who it was that she could trust. Literally one sentence could change everything she'd ever known.

"But he told me... that he also recently spoke with you."

Her neck and face grew hot again. He knew she'd spoken with him. Then again, he knew everything that happened to her back in college too, and the reason why she hated Jensen so much.

"I wasn't sure whether or not I could believe him— because I knew the history you had with him and how much you despised him. And then my mind began playing tricks on me. If you were speaking with him again, then I felt like you were lying to me. How long have you been lying to me?" His voice was intense and shaky.

Raine saw fearless, intense emotion building inside him. He was never one to blurt anything out. He usually played the hard guy routine, and this new and sudden burst of emotion scared her. She, at this point, was not entirely sure what he was capable of doing. Or of doing to her.

"I'd only just spoken with—"

"Shut up!" Marcus yelled.

She closed her eyes and let his words wash over her. She opened them again with hesitation and looked back up at his rage.

"He's working on a very important assignment. Research experiment. It's been going on for years. I know you're already aware of this. And he only needs one person to assist him. Or not even to assist, but to work alongside him, as equals."

She did already know this.

"Not you AND me. One person. And he's looking for me to prove to him that I'm a capable psychologist to work alongside."

She was beginning to understand the gist of the situation.

Her stomach was up in her throat like a lump at this point. The conversation she'd had with Jensen, he'd also had with Marcus.

And Jensen had pitted Marcus up against her.

It was either him, or her.

It had come down to this.

TWENTY

Raine Walsh

"This is ridiculous, Marcus, let me out!" Raine's well of emotion was filling with rage under her restriction. Marcus paced back and forth in front of the chair. "From the beginning... it's always been you. He doesn't want me. Why would he want me? What's so special about me?"

She watched him in a panic as he processed his own thoughts. Every moment he had to himself was even more and more dangerous for her. "C'mon. We can work together!"

He stopped and looked at her a moment, and her heart raced, then he looked away and she slumped back down.

"Can you at least tell me where we are?" she asked. She'd gotten a chance to look at the ground, and what she originally thought were rust stains on the uneven concrete, she thought for sure must be blood. It sent chills up her spine, and she became wary. How would Marcus have access to a place like this to begin with? He'd been kidnapped and brought here on Jensen's account? Who was the bald man? She just had so many questions and not enough time to ask them.

And then it hit her.

She remembered she'd had a mission as well when she left the vacation home. To prove to him that she was worthy and capable of being his partner, even though he'd been trying to get to her all these years. It was another form of manipulation.

This was the test. *This was it.*

He pitted her against somebody he thought she had feelings for. She needed to prove that she could get out of this. She couldn't help but feel a tad bit bad for Marcus as he was with his thoughts. He was probably thinking all the same things as her, only she knew the goal was to get out of this alive.

And he never answered her question about where they were. *How DID he have access to a place like this? What is above our heads?* She tugged at her restraints once more.

The problem was, she was tied to a chair and he was not.

It was also obvious that he was much stronger than her, proven by several breakouts throughout the course of their relationship—the most recent one being when she wanted information about why Alex came to see him.

"So what's going to happen now?" Her voice was low. He paced.

"Are you going to hurt me? Are you going to kill me?" The first question was already answered for her. He'd already hurt her to get her here. "That's the only surefire way for you to secure the job and you know it."

"Shut up!" he yelled again, advancing toward her.

She could have flinched, but she kept her composure, not even squinting at him coming into her personal space. She wanted to speak, and had so many things she wanted to say, but she didn't feel like that was what he wanted to hear right now. He had the upper hand.

Marcus leaned over onto her knees, breathing as though he were going to have a panic attack.

Despite everything, she thought about offering help.

"I know what I have to do," he said, his voice just above a whisper.

She wasn't sure what he meant. And despite knowing him all those years, she wasn't sure exactly what he was capable of doing.

"Listen carefully." His face was merely inches from hers. "He doesn't want me as his partner. He wants you. He's always wanted you. I'm not sure why... except that I know you're special." His voice cracked.

"Marcus don't," she said. He'd begun to enter his sulking phase—a phase she was familiar with.

"We just... we never got a chance to talk about us after you moved out," he said.

She sighed. She didn't want to talk about it. She didn't want to be strapped to a chair and forced to beat a dead horse.

"It was always about him, huh." His eyes quivered, a change in his face went from anger to weakness.

"Who, Jensen?" she spat.

"No."

There was a moment of silence in the basement, an eerie one with an echoing drop of water from one of the corners.

"It was always about Arie."

What does he want to hear... what does he want to hear? She racked her thoughts. "I'm sorry," she said, looking down. "I'm still really angry with you."

"Why? Can you at least give me that?" he asked.

"I don't want to talk about our relationship, yet now I'm strapped to a chair in front of you and forced to? That is not the right way to do this!"

"If we don't talk now, you'll never give me that closure!"

" Did you ever love me?" He whimpered.

She sighed. "Of course. We've been through a lot together. And people grow apart. I grew apart from you. I'm sorry. I'm sorry I felt that way. Sometimes you can't control your emotions, just like you couldn't control what happened to me, okay? We're all just humans." She looked around the basement. She was getting antsy. Where was the way out? "What my question is... is where in the world do we go from here?" she asked, hoping it was okay to ask that, knowing that he probably didn't even have that answer.

"Only one of us can leave this basement."

Her heart began to race in her chest.

"And it has to be you," he finished.

She exhaled slowly, shakily. "What do you mean?" she whispered.

He looked up into her eyes. "He wants you. It was you this whole time."

Her mind was racing and she studied his fiery, fierce pupils. She wasn't sure what he was planning to do or once again, what he was capable of doing.

"This is what is going to happen. I'm going to untie you from this chair. Then, you're going to hit me over the head with it and knock me out. Then, you're going to run out of here, do you hear me?" His voice was quiet and fast, so that it was an exchange that only the two of them heard, regardless if somebody was listening or not, which was always a possibility in this game.

Her chest rose and fell. "This is the only way?" she asked. "I could just say that I got away."

"That's the only way it looks real," he said. "Everything is a game here, Raine."

She nodded. She knew what he meant. "Won't he ask how I got untied? Why would you untie me?"

Marcus began to work the bonds on her legs from the posts on the chair, then stood up. "We could just say that Ray came down here and tried to rape you before I came down. The arms on the chair would make it hard for him to... err maneuver around, especially with your hands tied."

"Ray?"

"Bald headed guy."

She hated the thought. But it just might work. "Would Jensen buy that?"

"It's better than it actually happening." Instead of going around to the back of the chair to untie her wrists from the zip ties, he reached in his pocket and pulled out a pocket knife. He leaned forward, as though he were giving her a hug and reached behind her to cut off the zip tie. She turned her cheek away from his and closed her eyes. She did not want to be this close to him.

He leaned on her chest with his face right up against hers, and she caught a whiff of his aftershave. It smelled of memories. Good memories of feeling safe, and happy, and full. Memories that were long past the point they were at. And it gave her a flash of how far apart they were now. She turned back to him and allowed her cheek to touch his for just a moment. The zip ties were cut loose, but they stayed there, frozen a moment in time.

"You need to make it look like we had a struggle," he whispered into her ear as he placed the knife into the palm of her hand and closed her fingers around it. Then he backed away.

She looked down at the knife, suffocation lines around both wrists where the zip ties were so taut against her skin. One had torn into her, on the same hand as her burn, and that hand had gone numb. Through the pain, she moved it back and forth, hoping that she still had function.

Locking eyes with Marcus, she took the pocketknife up to her face and set it against her cheekbone, under her eye. She inhaled sharply before slashing it across her face. The knife flew from her hand and clanked on the ground as she reached up and held her cheek, blood seeping through her fingers. She looked up at Marcus, who had fear in his eyes. *What was she capable of?* Then, she stood and grabbed the chair.

"I will turn around so you can slam it on my back," he said, his voice shaking.

She didn't want to do this. She wrapped her fingers around the frame of the wooden chair.

Marcus looked back over his shoulder. "Oh, Raine?" he whispered.

She stopped and looked at him attentively.

"I know you'll do the right thing. But you must know. The research he's recruited you for..."

She held her breath.

"It's extensive experimentation into the suggestibility of hypnosis. Be careful."

She froze. This is the first time she'd heard this information and it sent her into a whirlwind of thoughts. Things in her mind connected from one end into the other. Things that didn't make sense before were latching together because of one sentence from Marcus.

And the last words he spoke, *be careful*, were chilling and almost a rule book in their own right. One that showed that he really did care about her and for her safety, even if he'd fallen into a rabbit hole. Marcus really was a good guy. He'd made many mistakes, but what human didn't? And she'd made a ton more mistakes than him.

"Just do it, Raine."

"There has to be another way..."

"Do it!" he yelled.

Tears rolled out of the sides of her eyes and down her cheeks, the salt in them stinging the cut she'd implemented on her cheek.

She needed to decide what was right and what was wrong with the professor. *Was he manipulating her this whole time? What was his involvement in trying to get to her all these years?*

She lifted the chair, which was heavier than expected and buckled a little of her shoulder.

"I'm so sorry," she said to Marcus, as she brought the chair down on him. His knees crumpled down to the floor, with his face turned, blood coming from his lip where he must have bit himself as he went down.

She didn't check to see if he'd passed out or not. But she dropped the chair onto the ground, hardly hearing its clang, and tripped toward the stairs. Using her hands to help guide her up the uneven steps, she pulled toward the stream of light under the door at the top.

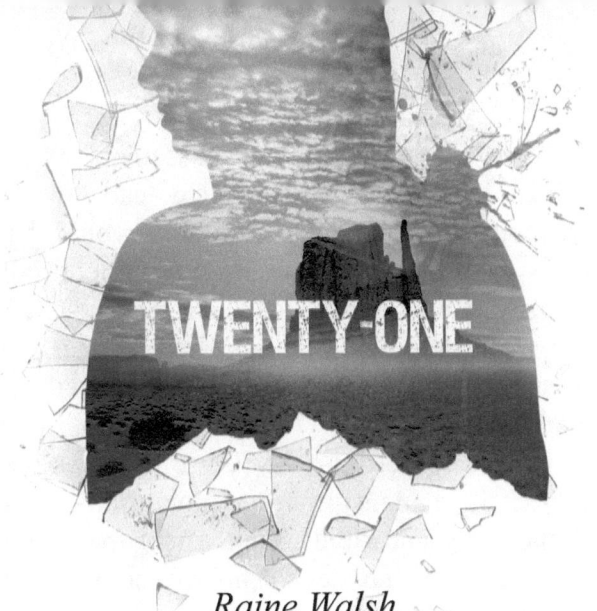

TWENTY-ONE

Raine Walsh

She creaked open the door to the basement and craned her neck back and forth. Ray was up here somewhere. He was the one who had treated her poorly when transporting her here.

Her adrenaline was pumping and when she didn't see anyone, she pushed open the door and fell out, careful not to put her hands everywhere and leave a trail of her blood behind. She fell into some sort of front foyer of a beautiful mansion. It seemed familiar, it smelled familiar, but she had never been here before. She found the door that had light coming through windows on both sides, and the one with the mail slot toward the bottom. That was her way out.

She stumbled toward the front door and twisted the knob open, looking over her shoulder to be sure that nobody was behind her. The sunlight pierced her eyes as she opened the door and she threw her forearm up to her head to shade her unadjusted eyes. In that instant, she recognized the porch, the yard, the street.

Because she had just been here not too long ago.

She was at Jensen's house.

That basement, was the same basement where Alex Wood's DNA was found which would lead law enforcement to reopen his hit and run case, which would then keep Jensen away from this residence. He wasn't here right now. He was at his vacation home. That cellar that she left Marcus in was the same basement that her client Tanner faced his own nightmare, having to fight and beat a person that looked exactly like him.

She wanted to get far away from that house. But the fact remained: She had no phone, no money, no car. She was bloodied and dirty and tired. She'd spent the entire night in that basement with no sleep. This mansion was close to the university, so perhaps she could go to Stanford for help, though she had no form of ID, nothing. Perhaps she could go to Lilly's office? That was the only place she felt was safe, though she wasn't sure how she was going to get around looking the way she did currently.

Whatever decision was made, she needed to get to the one person that she owed an apology to: Jonah Heely. Heely didn't bug her phone and track her. Marcus had. She'd shut him out and broke her ties with him, and he was probably the most helpful person to her. She'd been horrible to him, after everything he'd been through to help her. She couldn't believe how she'd let that happen, and the remorse was enough to cripple her right there on that porch.

Raine smoothed out her hair and walked down the street a little way, distancing herself from the mansion. She wasn't entirely sure where she was, except what little remained in her memory from being at that house when she'd come for Tanner. She cursed herself inside again for relying on her phone so much to get her where she needed to be, to the point where she couldn't find a location again. Or what was in the neighborhood for that matter. Though at the time, she didn't think she'd ever find herself coming back to this place to begin with.

Ahead, there were signs in the yard of a large house on the corner, announcing some university athletes lived there. She figured she'd take a shot and walked up to the door. She rang the doorbell and stood back.

A college-aged girl with blond pigtails opened the door wearing a baby blue fluffy bathrobe. She eyed Raine up and down with hesitation, and almost closed the door, but ended up just shutting it a little more to create a barrier between the two of them. "Can I help you?" she asked in a soft, wary voice.

"Hey, uhm. I'm sorry I know this is weird, but I had a bad night last night, uhh partying and I ended up in this neighborhood when I woke up. I don't have my purse or cell phone on me, and I'm pretty sure I got in a fight with a cat or something." She pointed to her cheek and laughed, acting as though she was just brushing it off. Raine felt like the girl who answered the door was worlds away from her, even though graduating college didn't seem so long ago. It seemed with every passing year she was older and older than the ones still in school.

The girl nervous laughed. "I understand *that*," she said, cracking a small smile.

Raine generally wasn't very intimidating, and she hoped she sounded natural saying that she was out partying. "Uhh, I was wondering if I could use your guy's bathroom and a phone to call my friend to pick me up?" she asked. It had been a long shot, but she had no other choice.

"Yeah, okay. Uh, hang on." She slammed the door.

Raine backed up on the porch, hugging the sides of her biceps with her hands and gave them a gentle rub. She hoped she wasn't being shut out just now, and the quivering behind her eyes twitched again, as though she might cry. That also could have been because of the sleep deprivation, but she was just going to hang out and see what happened.

A moment later, the door opened again. Two more girls stood with the blond pigtailed girl and they all peered out onto the porch. The one who looked older than the other two pulled back the door. "C'mon in. Courtney says you don't have a phone or anything?" she asked.

Raine shook her head. She was ushered inside by the girls.

"The bathroom is down the hall to your right. We're just in the kitchen having breakfast. Do you uhhh..." The girl looked her up and down.

Raine folded her arms over her chest, vulnerability washing over her.

"Do you want a change of clothes?" she asked.

Raine smiled, "That would be so nice. Thank you." she held her hand up to her chest in the region of her heart. She really was grateful that she'd been lucky enough to knock on this door.

Raine looked at her reflection in the bathroom mirror. The vanity was covered with beauty products and makeup. Her eyes were sunken and bloodshot. Her cheek was cut and blood stained down onto her shirt. She lifted her hand and touched the tender cut on her cheek that she gave herself. Marcus sacrificed his life for hers. Regardless how mad she was at him for all the things they'd been through in the past, when it came down to the end, he allowed her to escape and put himself in harm's way.

She didn't want to hit him. She wasn't a violent person by any means. And she saw that he had been manipulated by Jensen. What was she thinking? How had she gotten so suggestible that she'd actually begun to consider working with him? He'd manipulated her as well. And that was the part that hurt the most. She needed to get to the bottom of this. She needed to get to Heely's place to tell him everything she'd learned. And that last chilling sentence that Marcus told her, that Jensen was messing and playing with hypnosis. That was dangerous territory. Very dangerous.

She turned on the water and let it run over her hands. Blood and dirt swirled down the drain. Then she leaned over the counter and splashed the water onto her face. She exhaled, relieved to have the liquid trickle over her skin. She kept the water cool, which felt amazing on her burned hand. She continued to splash until there was a knock at the door. Her stomach flipped. She'd gotten lost in the moment and realized she was still in a strange house. "Yes?" she asked, fearful she'd hear a man's voice. The bald-headed guy. Or Jensen himself, even though he wasn't in the same state. Did she know that for sure?

"I have some clothes for you." The girl with the soft voice said through the door.

Raine grabbed the hand towel on the rack and patted her face dry, careful with her cut. She opened the door and stared blankly at the girl. The blond-haired pig tailed girl who was called Courtney stretched her arms out, a pair of black yoga pants and a black, cardinal, and white colored Stanford hoodie in her arms.

She took the clothes from her and smiled, then went to close the door.

"You look so familiar to me." Courtney said.

Raine looked at her again to see if she knew this girl from somewhere. She'd never seen her before.

"This may seem silly but... are you related to Chloe Walsh?"

Raine straightened her posture. "Chloe is my little sister," she said almost automatically.

Courtney smiled, placing her hand over her mouth.

"Are you friends with Chloe?" Raine asked.

"Yes, we're in the nursing program together. I thought you looked like her. Just a different color hair—"

"And older looking."

Both girls laughed.

"Naw, you could be twins. Is Chloe okay? She left so quickly to go back home. Are *you* okay?"

Raine was overwhelmed and felt warmed that this girl in front of her was an ally, and had known her sister, which made it such a small world. "Yes, to both questions I hope. Chloe's safe now." She didn't mean for it to sound so ominous, but she was so tired and couldn't think straight.

"You weren't really partying last night were you?"

Raine pursed her lips and stood a moment, holding the clothes like an idiot. She shook her head no, looking to the ground. She didn't want to explain anything further though.

"I won't tell the other girls if you don't want us to know what happened. It's okay." She gave another comforting smile. "But maybe you should let me look at your face? And... I noticed your hand as well." She nodded down to the red, chapped hand Raine held over the sweatshirt.

Her cheeks grew hot. Among other things, it was just embarrassing.

"Can I come in?" she asked.

Raine smiled in return and nodded, her eyes welling at Courtney's kindness. "I would appreciate that." She turned and walked back into the bathroom.

Courtney closed the door. She knelt down and fumbled underneath the sink cabinet for a moment. She pulled out some alcohol pads and gauze, then got back up and searched the countertop. Then Courtney reached between two bottles and pulled a bottle of green gel. "Aloe!" she said happily as she sideways glanced down at Raine's raw hand. "It's awkward because it doesn't really rub in. It's kind of greasy. But it'll be some relief while you're here and I take a look at that cut on your face. It'll do wonders to pull out the heat of a burn, as it did coming back from spring break in Cancun."

She had known it was a burn without Raine even telling her what the injury was. This girl was good. She wondered how far into the nursing program she was. She couldn't be any older than Chloe. And Chloe was a first year. She wondered how hard their classes were, or if maybe even this girl had experience outside of Stanford. Either way, Raine liked her. She approved of her friendship with her sister, if she had a say even, and she felt like she trusted her. Having been so good at identifying the burn, she wondered, though there was no way, whether or not she'd be able to determine what the cuts on her wrists were from. She knew Courtney saw them, but every time she looked, she'd quickly glance away like it was none of her business.

Raine took the bottle of aloe from Courtney's outstretched hand and squeezed a small bit of it out onto her burned hand. She used her other hand to spread it around, and then tilted her head back and exhaled a sigh of relief. The cooling sensation sunk into her skin and soothed, the best feeling she could possibly imagine. She looked up to see Courtney giving a small smile of validation.

Courtney lifted her chin gently, observing the cut on her cheek.

"It's fine. It doesn't even hurt..." Raine said, avoiding eye contact. She didn't want to tell Courtney, even though she wasn't prying by any means, that the cut on her face was self-inflicted. She was sort of upset about the fact that she didn't even need to do that to herself.

"Well it's definitely swollen. I'm not sure what caused this—" Courtney said, "...so in order to insure it doesn't get infected, I'd feel better cleaning it. You definitely don't need stitches, which is great."

Raine looked over to the counter where the alcohol pads were. This was definitely going to hurt. "All right."

Courtney reached over and grabbed the swabs.

She smelled the alcohol as it passed by her nose. She closed her eyes and breathed in, channeling the relief she felt on her hand.

"I'm sorry." Courtney cooed and then went in to dab Raine's face with the swab.

The sting was sharp. Penetrating through to her sinuses and the pressure point of her head. She kept her eyes closed as Courtney cleaned the cut. She'd need a story for it.

Courtney backed up and Raine opened her eyes. She was handed a towel for her greasy hands, and that's when Courtney looked down at her wrists and shifted again.

"Your hands were bound," she whispered, as though she was afraid to address the elephant in the room.

Raine looked down at the floor, searching her mind for an excuse.

"If you—and you don't have to tell me—but if you need help, there are hotlines, there are people that can help you. If you're in an abusive relationship..."

Raine couldn't quite figure out what she was talking about at first, but now it was making sense. She almost wanted to laugh, but that would have been highly inappropriate. But she also didn't want to explain what actually happened.

It also crossed her mind that this girl had no idea that she, sitting in front of her, was a clinical psychologist, unless Chloe had mentioned it at some point. But then again, Raine had no idea what their relationship was.

"I appreciate your kindness." Raine used her gentle, soft voice. "Really, if I could just use a phone I'd be okay. It's not what you think... but I'm okay now."

She nodded. "I understand." Then she took her cell phone out of her back pocket and handed it to Raine. "Clothes are there—" She nodded to the floor where Raine put the sweatshirt and pants. "And breakfast is in the kitchen with us if you're hungry. Just bring my phone back when you're done." She nodded and turned to leave.

Raine stood, "Courtney. Thank you. This means more to me than you know."

Without turning, Courtney nodded and then left the bathroom.

She changed her dirty clothing into the outfit laid out for her. It was comfortable, and she was grateful for it. Then she tossed her clothes into the small trash bin by the toilet. She picked up the cell phone and dialed the number that she knew by heart, thank god, better than any other number.

"Altor, Walsh, and Everstein's office, how may I direct your call?"

"Sylvie. It's me, Raine. Is Lilly in the office right now?"

"It's good to hear your voice. Yes, one moment."

The line went quiet as the call was transferred.

"Raine?"

"Lilly."

"Are you okay, what's going on?"

It seemed as though every conversation they'd had with each other lately involved anxiety and worry.

"Uhh, it's a lot to explain. I'm okay right now, but I was wondering if you could come pick me up?"

"Of course, where are you?" Lilly's voice sounded uneasy, but it was dripping with kindness despite the fact she was wary as to why Raine would call her over someone else.

"Well I don't know the exact address, but I can explain where the house is?"

"Anything'll work."

She explained the neighborhood and where she believed she was in reference to the university. She also said that if that wasn't enough, she could ask one of Chloe's friends for the exact address. Telling Lilly that she was with one of Chloe's friends eliminated the questioning for now. It was the easiest way to describe how she'd gotten where she was without going into much detail. Any amount of detail from her night and morning would prompt a thousand more questions, and Raine was to the point of emotional exhaustion that she just didn't have the brainpower to explain. Lilly seemed okay with it.

She hung up the phone and finished freshening up in the bathroom, then made her way out and shyly entered the kitchen where the rest of the girls were eating. She was welcomed to the table and food put in front of her.

She couldn't believe the amount of luck she'd endured after escaping where she just was.

When she thought about it, it had been one of the most terrifying betrayals of her life.

And she wasn't thinking about Marcus.

TWENTY-TWO

Detective Heely

J onah trudged up the steps to his apartment after a long night. It was quiet and eerie at three in the morning. He rubbed at his eyes as his head swirled. He was getting too old to be out late, or drinking late for that matter. He'd had a good time with his date, and though they'd had a good time back at the guy's apartment, Jonah didn't think it best to fall asleep there on their first date—not to say they didn't have fun before he left.

He wanted to go to sleep. But just like always, he simply couldn't get his work out of his mind. Seeing Marcus tonight, or last night, triggered some concern. It was such a weird encounter, and seeing him get into that vehicle, al-though it seemed like an afterthought, really bothered him.

He reached the landing and fumbled with his keys for the right one. It was a wonder he'd even made it to the cor-rect door, the way it took deep concentration to pin the key in the slot. He turned the key and pushed open the door, locking it behind. He yawned so large that he had to shut his eyes, and when he opened them again, his eyes fell on his wall mural, the reason he hadn't invited that nice guy back to his own apartment.

The thing was, he'd forgotten to update it after he'd gotten back from Stanford, and from going to Jensen's residence to see if he was there. There was a man at Jensen's residence that was defensive and sort of creepy. He didn't want Heely anywhere near the property. Perhaps that had something to do with all the law enforcement poking around recently, let alone the news stations.

But that wasn't why Heely continued to stare at the connections on the board. Yes, he needed to get that bald man up on the board, and he felt slightly bad for the guy for having been pinned in his head as *the bald guy*. Regardless, he was important. Not only because he'd seen him that day watching over Jensen's house, but because he'd seen him again. Last night.

He'd been the one arguing with Marcus. The one that tucked into the car quickly, but not fast enough. Jonah had seen him. And he had recognized him, even if it was only his subconscious at the time. That was the thing about Jonah's mind. He remembered everything, and everything was important.

Of course, all of this could be attributed to his tipsy, stupor headache that was emerging from lack of sleep and addition of multiple old fashioneds, and he hoped he'd remember it in the morning. He made a few notes on the wall, but knew that if he pursued it right now, nothing would be productive. No connections were being made in his mind right now—he needed a fresh, well-rested mind.

And right now, he'd be lucky if he made it to his bed in time.

Jonah woke up slowly, peacefully. Low, little rumbles and cracks in the sky outside the apartment resounded into his room, indicating the full-fledged thunder storm that hit outside. He yawned and stretched his arms up over his head without opening his eyes. He could lay in bed all day and listen to the storm outside. It was relaxing.

And then it hit him. The thoughts he'd had right before he fell asleep, still fresh in his mind. Still taunting.

He jolted out of bed and hurried into the family room, in just his boxer shorts. His head took a moment to catch up to his movement, and when it did, it pounded pain into his skull. He clamped his teeth together and shut his eyes until the throbbing subsided. He was way too old to be drinking and staying up that late. Nothing that a little orange juice and aspirin couldn't cure, he hoped. After he regained composure, he straightened his spine and stared at the wall.

The markings were still there from last night. The bald-headed guy and where his connections lay on the board. Jonah hadn't been dreaming it, like he thought for a split moment. He instantly regretted the fact that he didn't have access to the database he used to, or he would have already run the man's identity through the system. However, he didn't have anything to run even if he could convince an old friend or his father to follow through with it against procedure, which was a long shot. He didn't have the guy's name, and he didn't have any form of ID or DNA either. You can't look somebody up by just their description.

Without even looking up this man, he knew that he had a connection to somebody he was familiar with besides Dr. Dill Jensen. *Marcus.* That's where he needed to start. He searched around for his cell phone, forgetting where he put it a moment. It was unusual that he ended up finding it on the sink in the bathroom, which he had no recollection of, though last night was a weird whirlwind. He clicked on the saved number and waited.

"Walsh, Altor, and Everstein's office. How many I assist you?"

"Hi there. Dr. Altor please."

"May I ask who's calling?" The woman seemed almost as though she was a recording, her voice perfectly cadenced.

Should he say it was him? Should he tell her he was a PI? He didn't want to cause alarm. Or did he?

"Jonah Heely," he decided on the truth.

"And are you a patient of his?"

Wow, this lady is nosy. "I am... not. But I need to get in touch with him immediately." Now that he thought about it, he could picture who this woman was. He remembered seeing her when he was in their office, speaking with Raine a while back. She wasn't going to let him through, that much was clear.

"I will write down your information and have him get back to you at his earliest convenience."

Something in her voice wasn't right. It wavered, something he'd never heard in this receptionist's voice before. *She was lying.* Or, she wasn't sure she was telling the complete truth. What was this all about?

"Ma'am. If I don't speak to him right now, I'm going to drive down to the office and speak to him in person. I'm a... I'm a private investigator—" The title was still fresh on his mouth, "and I need to have a word with Marcus. It's very important."

There was a pause. "I would love for you to speak to him, *Private Investigator* Heely, but Marcus has been gone from the office for several days now. And... we don't know where he is."

That explained her weird behavior. And the fact that she may indeed be worried about this. But he wasn't entirely missing now, was he? Jonah saw him last night. And he seemed fine until the end of the night when he was loading into that car with bald man. Bald man... who was connected with the professor in one way or another.

"Thank you for your time and information, er,"

"Sylvie."

"Sylvie. I appreciate your kindness," he was about to hang up, but had another thought. "Is Raine there?" He asked, unsure if it was a smart idea.

There was hesitation on the line. "She, too, has taken a leave of absence. Don't you have her personal number?"

He gathered this receptionist on the other end of the line might have more information about him than he imagined she did. "I do... I'll call her there. Thanks." He hung up with Sylvie and sat for a moment. He would not call her personal line.

His attention was drawn to the map again. The answers were right there. He was so sick of staring at this thing when the pieces were not speaking to him. It took moments before thinking through the information he found last night and this morning, and then matching it up with his map.

Marcus had been absent from his job. Raine took some kind of leave. Marcus was seen last night at the club, looking distressed. The guy that was with him was the same guy he'd ran into at the professor's residence.

He began to put two and two together. Perhaps...Jensen was at his vacation home. He wasn't here and that much was clear. Raine could be with him. Perhaps the bald-headed guy was instructed to bring Marcus to them.

In that case... Marcus *was* in trouble.

It wouldn't hurt to try and get a hold of Raine. See if she was actually at the professor's vacation home. He pulled his phone back out and dialed her cell number. It rang a few times before it went to voicemail.

Go figure. No answer. The more moments he sat on the couch, the more he'd fully convinced himself that she was at the center of this. She always was. She always had an 'in', with every case that he'd been involved with since meeting her. She was the connection, without a doubt. The answer he was searching for. It was so clearly right there in front of him.

And if he didn't act now, another victim would emerge, and she would get off unscathed, again.

Well not on his watch.

The first case he was going to solve as a private investigator would be the one that he'd been obsessing about for months on end. He leaped off the couch and rounded the apartment for his things. His gun. His phone. What else he would need. It was like he was a kid and was just told by his parents that he could spend the night at his friend's house. He was excited, running around the apartment and gathering the essentials.

And as he rushed to the door, he realized one thing.

He was still in his boxers.

TWENTY-THREE

Detective Heely

Jonah pressed the gas pedal into the floor as the car engine revved down the sanded desert road. The sky was already dark, which was better for him because he would have more cover. Something strange was going on inside him, that he didn't expect when he embarked on this trip. With every moment in time he got closer to his destination, his apprehension grew. It was as though something was telling him not to do it.

To turn around.

As a detective, he had been always running toward the fire. Never away. That was the part that gave him adrenaline. He wondered if his experiences, especially the close call at the stadium, had made him "soft"— something his father would call him growing up.

Only right now, there was something to say for intuition. And his intuition as he neared the vacation home of Professor Dill Jensen, was screaming at him that something was not right.

The GPS on his phone said the house was located just a mile ahead, which was hard to believe because there was nothing but desert around, and darkness for miles. He even felt vulnerable with the headlights of his car blaring out in front of him.

Because the phone told him he was so close, he veered off the road and into the sand. He was going to have to trek the rest of the way to the house on foot. If he was going to be discreet, that was the only way. And he wanted to catch Raine and Jensen in the act of whatever they were doing with Marcus before he stepped in and saved the day.

He closed the door to his car with a gentle click, and even just that slight movement felt like it echoed off the canyons. He double-checked his pants for his phone, his gun, his car keys. Everything was secured. Then he set off on foot down the road. The house was just around the bend.

He'd already begun to break a sweat, under his arms and at his hair line. He brushed his brow with his forearm as he rounded the hill and saw the lights to the large home. He stepped off the road into the desert foliage that surrounded the house and moved stealthily.

It'd been more than once that he found himself hiding in shrubbery, and the very instance reminded him of when he was hiding in Vinnie's bushes, trying to catch *him* in the act as well. That outing didn't quite go as planned, if he remembered correctly, and he thought about the consequences of his actions now as well.

Should I call for back up? he asked himself. Then he remembered. He had no back up. Nothing of an official capacity, for certain. Before, he could call in a favor to the station. Now, it wasn't his station. He still had friends there, but they weren't technically his coworkers now. Perhaps he should just call the police and request them send someone out here. But then, that might mess up his plan.

What would happen if he DID catch something shady going on though? What could he do? One man? Was this the smartest thing? *I really shouldn't be doing this.* The intuition was burning now.

But something else inside him told him he was *so close*. So close to solving all the mysteries that haunted him since the day he met the psychologist. And that alone was enough for his brain to turn off every red flag that presented itself in front of his nose.

There was no stopping now.

He'd come too far.

He'd waited too long.

The time was now.

He moved through the trees, closer to the terracotta colored structure. As he placed his back against the house, he inched his way forward. The front porch was just there, around the corner. He peered around, and his breath caught in his throat. To his surprise, it looked as though the front door was wide open. He blinked, hard, shutting his eyes and opening them again, allowing them to adjust to the darkness once more to see if what he'd seen was a hallucination. Was this a mistake—leaving the door open? Was it his opportunity?

Once again, the red flags. Of course. Why wouldn't those alarm bells be blaring in his mind? This could be a setup. A trap.

He moved forward. How would they even know he'd followed them out here? Why would they be trying to bait him?

He couldn't do this alone. He needed back up. He pulled out his phone. The light on the screen was brighter than he'd intended, and he extinguished the beam to his shirt for a moment, before pulling it away and bringing up his contacts. He was going to call the police. He looked up at the wide door again, but then it dawned on him.

Perhaps they were not baiting him to come into the house.

Perhaps, they had already come out.

And whoever 'they' were, he was right. He felt their presence behind him. Turning to face the person, he was greeted by a painful blow to the head. His neck creaked, sending him flying backward, off balance. He hit the ground, hard, lights spinning in his mind. He tried to catch a glimpse of who it was. This intruder. But wait... *he* was the intruder.

His thoughts became spaced out. His vision grew dark.

TWENTY-FOUR

Detective Heely

T here was a throbbing pulse that pounded just above his right eyebrow. A hot, sticky substance caked the side of his face. *Sweat?* Naw, this was thicker. *Blood?* It was blood. He moved his hand to reach up and wipe it, but his hand was stuck. Locked. That's when he felt his arms aching, throbbing with his head. He wanted to move but couldn't.

When his eyes focused, he realized he was on the ground, restraints looped onto hooks set in the concrete. The floor was cool and glazed. He was in some sort of garage. He looked to the left and right, noticing some chalky substance surrounding him, though he couldn't quite make out what it was.

Wherever he was, he did not have the upper hand.

He was bound.

Vulnerable.

Injured.

He tried to lift his head to see around the room, but every time he moved his neck, he was hit with insurmountable pain. He gritted his teeth and yanked at the wrist and ankle restraints once more. "What kind of sick game is this?" he managed to mutter the words on his copper tasting tongue.

"You're awake."

He craned his neck to see who spoke. It was a man's voice. *Not Marcus.* Not one he recognized. It took him a moment to realize the voice came from above. He lifted his chin to the ceiling to catch a glimpse.

"Where am I? What happened?" he croaked. *The car. The desert. The shrubbery.* He had reached for his phone. For backup. This was Dr. Dill Jensen's vacation home.

"You were snooping. This is private property."

"I— I was looking..." He shut his mouth. Neither Raine nor Marcus were in sight. Perhaps he'd made the biggest mistake of his life. Was Raine hiding in some other room? Was this professor the pregame show?

"You've been snooping for quite a while, Detective. Don't act like this is a new development."

He didn't know what to think. How to feel, except drained. Defeated.

The old man continued, "...at my place of employment... at my residence... *here.* And what is it you think you're going to find?"

Well he could answer that loud and clear now. But an hour ago he had been looking for something else. *Someone* else. "You have the wrong idea. I was not working on the case that took place at your house." It was all he could think to say to refute against the accusations, even if they were true.

He was quiet a moment. "What ARE you working on then? Not that it matters. I'm just curious."

Jonah didn't want to answer. He was embarrassed now. He wasn't sure he wanted to blow Raine's cover. All along his notes pointed to her working with this guy. He didn't have complete and total proof that she still wasn't but also, it wasn't her that had him tied down right now. And Raine had tried to come to him multiple times with information that led these cases back to this man, the notorious professor. And he never listened. Nobody listened to her about this. He thought she was trying to find a cover. Or anything that made sense to her because of the vulnerable state she was in.

"Normally I don't do these kinds of things, Detective."

Jonah tried to swallow and lubricate his dry, sore throat. This didn't feel like amateur, first time crime.

"Normally I have someone else do the dirty work. Somebody willing. Someone more motivated to do so. Motivated to please."

"Please who?" The words slipped out.

"Me."

"What else have you done?" It was a long shot, asking. But that was always the start. And the dangerous thing was, that question was a complete risk to his safety. If Jensen told him what he'd done, the chances of him getting out of this situation alive were next to none. The question was weighted, with all the answers lying at its end. What difference did it make if he got a confession? Was it more for his own peace of mind? If he was going to die, right here and right now on this garage floor, then he'd rather die knowing the truth. Right?

The man squatted next to his face. He appeared much more limber than Jonah would expect a man of his age to be. This man was not to be underestimated.

"You want to know what else I've done?" His voice didn't falter. It was confident. Cocky, almost. He was proud of his work.

"I've reinvented multiple psychological experiments from history, and I've done a better job of it."

Everything. He'd been at the bottom of everything. Every case Jonah had worked on in the past several months was orchestrated. Every case on the wall of his apartment.

Dr. Dill Jensen was the Mastermind Murderer all along.

"My most recent... was Brody Cross."

That was a name that Jonah didn't recognize. Was it a case that happened while he was on leave?

The old man must have seen the confusion on his face because he clarified, "You may know him more clearly as Tanner."

His body vibrated with that newfound knowledge. Brody Cross must have been the man that impersonated Raines client, Tanner. The one that mysteriously passed away in the hospital. Passed away... or murdered. The weight of this information sank on top of his chest. He was doomed. He was not leaving this room.

"Now, you are the only one that knows this. And you can help no one."

"Raine knows. And she will destroy you." He spat the words through his teeth. But he was becoming weaker. He knew no matter what happened to him, Raine destroying the professor was the truth. Because she had destroyed him. Unintentionally of course. But he'd focused so much on her and her involvement with the case, that it led him into a delusional mudslide that ended here. On this concrete. He'd lost directions and followed a path that led him to try and prove something that was never there.

He tried to move again, but with his wrists and ankles tied, it was no use. As he moved, he remembered the mess of chalk that surrounded him. "What is..."

"It's a chalk outline of you. I thought I'd be courteous and start the crime scene investigators job early for them. Make it a little easier."

He burned up inside. Jensen was mocking him. Mocking his authority, his position. Showing him that he was powerless. Something each one of his victims no doubt experienced. Something Raine had experienced, for which he'd never given her the benefit of the doubt.

He imagined his father walking into this room, after he was gone, whatever was going to happen to him, and looking down at the chalk line surrounding his sons' lifeless body. A single tear slipped out of the crease in his eye and rolled down the side of his face.

This was it.

And he hoped, after everything he'd become in his life, he hoped someone would be proud of him for the work that he had done.

TWENTY-FIVE

Raine Walsh

"I really appreciate you picking me up, Lilly." Raine told her from the passenger seat.

"Anytime. You were there for me when I needed you at the office." She did not take her eyes off the road. "Raine. Some weird things have been happening lately."

"You're telling me." Then it occurred to her that maybe Lilly had more information than she knew. "You mean about Marcus?" she asked. She felt a lump in her throat at the mention of his name coming from her lips.

"Well that too, the fact that we haven't seen him at all with no warning."

Raine knew where he was. Well... she *did*. Who knew what happened after she'd left?

"But what I meant was, that detective you used to work with has been trying to reach you at the office."

"Heely?" she asked. This was surprising. Why would he be wanting to reach out to her after the last phone call she had with him? Something must have happened. "Did he say what he needed?"

"No. But he did ask me for an address, and I gave it to him. I'm not sure if I should have."

"What address..." She was afraid to ask. "Lilly!"

"Jensen's vacation property."

Raine's heart dropped into her stomach. "You have to take me to his place. Please. I have to check if he's there. I don't have my phone on me."

"You know where he lives?"

"I asked one time when we worked together. His apartment is down the road from that street taco shack."

Lilly veered off their course down another road, changing direction entirely.

When they got to the complex and Lilly parked outside, Raine turned in her seat to face her. "I will be right back. I just need to check and see if he's here. If he's not... this could be bad, okay?"

"What's going on, Raine?"

"I don't have time to explain."

"I've been patient this whole time, not asking questions, supporting you. But this is crazy!"

"Lilly. It's bigger than you think. Okay? This is a matter of life and death."

"For who?"

Raine wished she could answer that question. She didn't want to think about it. She opened the car door and slipped out, "I'll be right back." She slammed the door and hurried across the lot and up the stairs. She looked around the doors until she came to the number she recalled him telling her was his apartment, and the address she remembered seeing on the false autopsy that she thought belonged to Brandon Perez at the time.

She wrapped her fist on the door and stood back.

No answer.

"Heely!" She banged her fist again, this time putting her ear up to the door to listen for any movement. "C'mon."

Nothing. He wasn't home. She partly knew that already.

But still, she had to see for sure. Knowing it was a long shot, she rattled the door knob and pushed into it. The door to the apartment was unlocked. She nearly fell inside and had to catch her footing.

A PI would never leave his residence unlocked. Heely'd been in a hurry.

She peered inside. "Heely? Are you home?"

No response. She looked back and forth before slipping inside his apartment and closing the door. She turned around, looking for any sign of struggle. She was worried she'd find him perhaps in the bedroom or bathroom, knocked out or worse... If Jensen knew Heely was onto him, it was only evident Jensen would find him first, she was sure of that. She turned around and walked into the family room.

Then, froze.

Her eyes wide, she stared at the fixture on the wall. Spread across the entire wall. The mind map. The bane of Heely's existence. She couldn't believe her eyes, and her body tensed with every detail she absorbed. The names, the places, the photos, the evidence.

Her name. Plastered everywhere.

She was so overwhelmed that she couldn't grasp exactly what she was looking at.

The door creaked behind her, and she nearly leaped out of her skin.

"Raine...?" The soft, mousy voice called out to her.

She turned to face Lilly, her face flushed and white as a ghost.

"What in the...?" Lilly had just noticed the wall behind her.

She watched Lilly squinting at the map, drawing closer to it. She turned back to the wall again and moved closer as well. Each case she'd been involved in, every nightmare of her life was laid out on the wall of Heely's apartment.

Only something was wrong. Completely wrong. This image was skewed. Heely had solved his map. It was complete. He'd identified someone he labeled as the 'Mastermind Murderer' on the map of all the cases, connected to each other. Only according to Raine, he'd pinpointed the wrong person.

Every red line pointed back to her.

To her understanding, if she replaced herself with the one person she'd suspected pretty much the entire time, the person whose trap Heely had likely fallen into, this entire map made perfect sense. No wonder her relationship with Heely fell to the wayside. While she was losing her trust with him over him tracking her and standing on the side of who she thought was her ex-boyfriend, Heely was cooking up a false truth of his own.

He thought SHE was the Mastermind Murderer.

She turned toward Lilly again. "It's not... this isn't true." She shook her head, her limbs beginning to shake, her knees buckling.

"Hey..." Lilly started toward her as though she'd be there to catch Raine, only she was awkward, holding her arms out and dropping them again. "I don't believe this, Raine." She motioned to the wall. "I believe you. I know this isn't true." Her voice shook. "But... what does this mean exactly?"

"It means that Heely is in trouble," she whispered.

"What do we do?"

"I need to go to Jensen's vacation home."

"I sent him there," Lilly whispered, her lip beginning to quiver. "I sent him into harm's way."

"No, he did this on his own. This was not your fault. But we are the only ones that know where he is. I need to go down there."

"I don't know if that's a good idea, Raine."

"Jensen... he thinks we're partners. Me and him. He doesn't know what I know. He'll trust me."

"Partners?" She squeaked.

"It's... a long story. Ugh, I wish I could tell you now! I will, I promise Lilly. But right now, I just need your help."

"Anything. Take my car."

Raine contemplated it. "That would be great."

"What else?"

"Can you tell Arie?"

She nodded.

"I lost my phone and I haven't been able to get ahold of him."

"I can do that. Go." Lilly handed out her keys to her. "I'll catch the bus."

Raine held her hand up to her chest. She was so grateful for this woman in front of her, the woman who she'd gotten off on the wrong foot to the wrong start. She never imagined they'd be where they were now. She turned and looked at the wall once more.

In the moment, she didn't have time to think about the depth of meaning in this wall. The true meaning. The fact that the professor was at the head of all that had happened to her. She stared at the wall as though to burn it into her mind, so that she could think about it on the drive down there.

All the killers had something in common with each other. The Warden, Vinnie, Tanner Copycat... they all went to Stanford University. So did she. They all had some kind of connection back to Professor Dill Jensen. So did she..."Oh my God... The club!" Raine whispered, out of breath, the synapses in her brain connecting things that hadn't made sense to her, ever.

Heely didn't know about the exclusive alumni club. The club that pushed the limits of psychology and experimentation. The fact that each case she'd been involved in since the day of her capture, had something to do with mimicking psychological experiments from history. The Stanford Prison Experiment. The Kitty Genovese case. The Milgram Experiment, with Alex being the unfortunate victim. Or the fact that Jensen had been trying to get her to be involved for years, even back when she was a student, nearly blackmailing her into it.

And the purpose of Chloe's kidnapping. It was all adding up now. She'd been manipulated into almost partnering with Jensen in his grand experiment. *How long has he been manipulating me?* The implications of Marcus telling her that Jensen was researching hypnosis began to all make sense now.

"Raine?"

She jumped as she turned away from the wall, toward Lilly again. She hadn't realized she had spaced out.

"You don't have to do this. You don't need to be a hero. We can call the police and let them deal with it. I'm serious. In fact, we *should* do that."

She considered it. That seemed the easy way out, right? But it wasn't. It was the complicated way, where she'd received no answers, and would be pushed to the wayside like she had been time and time again. "I have to. I have to see his face when he realizes his facade is over. I have to understand why. I cannot leave this stage of my life on a cliffhanger." She took the car keys from Lilly and headed for the door.

"Call me from Heely's phone when you get there. So Arie and I know you're safe."

She nodded.

"And Raine?"

She turned and looked over her shoulder.

"Should I stay away from Marcus?"

Raine thought about it a moment. He, too, was a victim. He let her go. Her heart hurt to think about him lying knocked out on the basement of the professor's house, not knowing what would happen when the bald man would come back, and what he would do when he saw that Marcus had lost— even though it was a set up.

"Yes, I believe you can trust him," she said quietly, leaving the apartment behind.

Leaving the wall, now etched in her memory, behind.

She was going to end this once and for all.

TWENTY-SIX

Raine Walsh

There was no hiding her car this time as she pulled into the driveway of the desert vacation home. Jensen thought she was on his side. And according to his map, Heely expected her to be there.

Her heart pounded, every limb in her body tense. She didn't know what she'd say to either of them, or what the situation would be when she walked into it. She had to prepare for anything and everything.

Though if she'd learned anything in life, it was that some things you just couldn't prepare for. She jumped out of the car, not even sure if she'd shut the door or not, and headed for the walk to the front of the house. She briefly thought about the fact that she should go into the back of the car and grab the tire iron or something. Always arm yourself. Only, she also knew that her mind had always been her best and strongest weapon. And in this current circumstance, her mind may be the only weapon she could conceal without causing alarm.

Only then, her attention was caught by a light at the end of the driveway. Perhaps instead of going right up to the door, she should follow the light. She hurried around a tree and toward the light, realizing it was the garage, with the door risen. As she approached the garage and looked around, the hump on the floor caught her attention.

Immediately her stomach caught into her throat. "Heely!" She rushed to his side and tugged at the iron restraints that held his wrists and ankles to the floor. Should she be surprised? Jensen was capable of anything.

She'd seen it.

She'd experienced it. He'd been masked the entire time, but nothing was secret now. It was all out in the open.

"Are you real?" Jonah breathed, his eyes wide under the crusty, busted skin. His face was bloodied. He'd been beaten.

She went into panic mode, looking around the garage for something to pry him up with, but also not wanting to leave his side. She couldn't leave his side. "Yes, yes, I'm real. It's me."

It suddenly occurred to her that she was still the enemy he came here to catch. But when she saw the look of terror in his eyes, and the relief at her presence, that told her otherwise. He'd met the real enemy.

"There's not— much time," he choked.

She didn't know whether he meant there wasn't much time before something else was going to happen, much time to escape, or much time before he couldn't breathe anymore.

"I saw your map—"

"I was wrong."

She nodded, her eyes welling. "I'm sorry I gave you that impression. I never—"

"I know. I know it was him all along."

She began to cry, the feeling elating her and overwhelming her at the same time. Someone, finally, the one who mattered most of all, the one most intimate in all of the cases she'd been subjected to, finally believed her.

And she needed to save him.

"He's coming back," he said.

The statement sent chills down her spine, and her anxiety flared up again.

"Save yourself," he choked again.

"No! I won't leave without you."

"Raine. I'm done. I know it. You know it. If you get out of here alive, you can help so many other people, as I failed to do."

"You didn't fail. Don't think that." She couldn't tell if he was choking on his own blood, or if what she'd said made him emotional. She couldn't give up on him. "You are a great detective, Jonah. And a great friend." She swallowed at the lump in her throat.

Just then, a spotlight shined around the corner.

Her head raised in alarm, and she squinted into the headlights of the car. She recognized it as Heely's car. She looked down at him in question.

"Go."

She read his lips as he closed his eyes. She shook her head 'no' as the engine of the car in front of her revved. On instinct, she stumbled backward, nearly tripping over her own legs. She pressed herself up against the wall of the garage, covering her mouth.

It all happened so fast.

The car rushed forward into the garage, rolling over the man in front of her.

Over Jonah Heely.

Raine crumpled to the hard, cold concrete.

THE DOMINO EFFECT

TWENTY-SEVEN

Raine Walsh

For a moment she thought she should run. But then, what would Jensen do if she did that? Would he run her over with Heely's car also without a second thought?

Heely's car.

Heely.

Life was so fragile.

Hers was too.

The old man turned off the car and stepped out, one foot after the other. He didn't even look at the scene behind him as he advanced toward Raine.

She put up her hands as if that were enough to stop him. "I told you I'd join your stupid club!" she spat, as though this was punishment for her not accepting sooner.

She thought she saw a hint of a smile on his cracked, pale pink lips.

"Join it? You already have."

The sentiment was bone chilling. He was right and she knew it. She'd been manipulated for years now, thinking she had control when this entire time, control was an illusion.

"And anyway, I'm sorry you had to see that, but you are going to have to get used to it if you'll be working with me. He was a threat to the study."

"Oh, like Alex Wood was?" She couldn't help herself.

With everything she said, he appeared to become more amused. She could hardly believe she was holding a conversation with him.

"Can we go inside and chat?" he asked. This monster's disposition was completely calm after he'd just brutally crushed a man.

She hesitated. If she went in there, she probably wasn't coming back out. And at this point, did she want to? *She had to.* Even if it was for everyone else who suffered at the hands of the professor, who she couldn't save prior. And now she needed to live to honor the memory of the private detective who only wanted to do the right thing.

She forced herself forward toward the door of the house, at her own will. She was playing it by ear, lucky that he hadn't drugged her or tied her up. She must not have been a threat to him, like the others were. But why? Why was he so trusting of her? Didn't he hear the words coming from her mouth, feel the energy she gave off?

She felt him behind her, closer than she wanted. Without asking, she headed straight for the room they were in last time, the office of sorts. He didn't correct her, so she plopped herself down on the couch. What could she possibly do now?

Use your mind, Raine. Use the power you know you have. If everything on Heely's map was true, observed with the perspective of Jensen's name in place of hers—then she was standing in the presence of a very dangerous man, all together made more real by the fact that it was verified.

"So, if I had joined your alumni club all those years ago in college, I would be just like any of the other murderers? I'd be dead."

"I don't think you would. They are dead because they were caught."

"They kidnapped other people. Murdered other people. How does this not bother you!?" She was a clinical psychologist, but she'd never worked with clients who were mass murderers, or mass manipulators. This wasn't her expertise, and he had the upper hand on her in knowledge and experience. Though one question remained, something she'd sincerely thought about and did not understand: his motivation for putting his life's work into this. Did she think she'd get a clear answer? No. But it was worth a shot.

He said, "You're a psychologist. You should understand why the work is so important. Because it defines so much about humanity that is hidden. So much that must be brought to light."

She was not the one to work with clients with these particular tendencies, but she did know somebody who was good at it. And he was also dead. Troy. Was he also a victim? It was something she hadn't considered before now. "Did you... kill Troy?"

"No." He smirked.

She hated the face he made.

"Allen did."

The Warden.

Well she knew that, but was it the Warden's idea to do this?

"Troy Batterman was dangerously close to finding you and ruining the entire experiment. He was also *in love* with you."

What did that have to do with anything? And he wasn't. She knew that. He was a womanizer. A charmer. He was by no means in love with her. But this brought up another tendency she hadn't considered in the professor. She'd felt it in the past. *Jealousy. Was he jealous?* He'd come onto her when she was in college. That one night in his office... She was frightened. She needed to protect herself.

Stay focused. Bring the conversation back to the point again. "But why mimic cases from history?"

"Because they must not be forgotten."

His logic was twisted. Pessimistic of society, and the human experience. But to him, it was right. It was uncovering the truth no matter the consequences.

Raine's attention was drafted over to a shelf, where emissions were being released from a machine. She recognized it as a diffuser of essential oils. But she didn't like this smell. It left a sour taste in her mouth, a sickly feeling in her stomach. It made her dizzy. She wondered if she was being drugged, familiar with his tactics now that she was fully aware he was at the bottom of this.

She wondered if it was getting to him as well. His eyelids were half closed, his breathing slowed. It didn't matter that he was old and she could probably physically take him. He had the power to control inside his mind.

"Are you feeling tired?" he asked. His voice had slowed to a cadence deeper than normal.

She recognized the smell, but she didn't know where from. Though it did remind her of a time in her life. The scent memory. Perhaps it was the smell he used in his office back at the university when she'd visited him. Because her mind kept fluttering right back to that time.

She nodded. She *was* feeling exhausted.

Just where he wanted her. Highly suggestible.

The hypnosis.

He'd done it in the case of Alex Wood, which explained why Alex felt like he'd dreamed all the things that happened to him. Marcus was able to identify this in his session with Alex.

If Marcus hadn't told her about this, she may have been in too deep, in this office with this dangerous man sitting across from her. Now that she was highly aware that he used the technique of hypnosis, she could be aware of this highly suggestible state.

And she decided to play along with it.

She wanted to see how far he'd take it. How far he thought he could take her to the point of suggestibility. Perhaps finally get what he wanted after all these years.

She felt hazy, but she just let it happen. She didn't know what he wanted, and she had to play it carefully. She remained quiet, staring at him across the room, waiting for him to make the move.

"Oh how I've missed you, Fran," he said, his face screwing up and his voice going limp.

Fran? He must think I'm someone else.

"I've... missed you too," she whispered. She was playing a dangerous game but needed to know how she was related to this Fran he spoke of.

"Why did you leave me?"

Once again, dangerous territory. This girl that Raine reminded him of, left him. They were in a romantic relationship? Many years ago? Perhaps.

This was why he was attracted to Raine all these years. Obsessed and needing her involvement in his research. They must have been partners.

She stood up, and he flinched as though he'd seen a ghost. She moved closer to him, her own body shaking like a leaf underneath her bravery. She had to get close enough to impair him. When she was within his grasp, he patted onto his knee for her to sit on his lap. She hesitated, but tried not to show it, so that he wouldn't be alerted that she wasn't under his hypnosis.

She forced herself onto his lap, his arm and hand touching the small of her lower back. His gentle touch sent a cascade of sickly chills throughout her body, yet she remained calm.

She turned her chest and leaned into him, as though she were giving him a hug. She placed her arms around him and hugged his neck. Her eyes darted behind his chair, which was up against his desk, that had things strewn about.

And then she saw it. The silver sheen caught her gaze. She leaned forward a little more, pushing into him as she carefully scooped up the letter opener that sat there in front of her.

"I'm not Fran," she whispered right into his ear, so close she felt his hair on her cheek.

"What?" he asked shakily, as though he was already losing himself.

"My name is Raine Walsh. I am not, and have never been who you think I am." She leaned back and brought her hand forward, the letter opener closed tightly in her fist. She used it to stab down into his thigh, flesh ripping at her touch. She yanked it back out quickly as he shrieked.

She dropped from his lap and scrambled backward as he doubled over in pain. She held the dripping, now crimson letter opener up by her face in her fist. "And I am NOT a murderer. But that doesn't mean I can't badly injure you until authorities get here and I can prove to them everything that Detective Heely found out about you. *Everything* about you."

Jensen looked up from his pained, heaving breath. The sheen still in his eye. "You mean everything the detective found out about you? He set it up perfectly for me."

So he HAD been to Heely's apartment. He knew all along that Heely was making a case against Raine. And now Heely was dead, so he couldn't prove her innocence after all.

This was bad for her.

He heaved and then spoke again, "And then you found out that he knew it was you... so you came here... and you killed him."

"No!" she yelled.

He flinched at her outburst. "Look, I'm an old man. I can't go on like this... but you... you can. You can finish the work. I never wanted you to just be another member of the club. I wanted you to take over my place. I thought... I thought Fran would take my place when I was gone."

"Well I'm not Fran!" she yelled again.

He nodded, his eyes glassy. "That much you have shown me," he whispered, so sinisterly and finite.

It was at that point that the old man, injured, advanced at her. He grabbed her neck with his bony hands.

She thrashed backward, losing her footing but being held up by the grip of his hands on her neck. She choked, batting at his hands with her own.

He was quick for his age and wounded leg, and she should have been ready for it. She tried to punch and the letter opener fell, clattering to the ground. Just as she felt her breath choked off, the door to the office burst open. She saw the professor's eyes bulge from his head, veiny and blood-shot. She heard voices and shouts behind her but could not quite make them out. All she knew was that just when the world was beginning to grow dark, she was released, heaving air as Jensen fell backward.

Raine was hoisted up by someone on either side of her and dragged out into the hallway. She heaved more fresh air, free from the diffuser that held onto her. She looked up to the sides of her, Arie on one side, Lilly on the other. Arie had bent down and scooped her up, carrying her out of the house into the front yard, and sat in the grass with her draped over her arms.

She balled into his chest. She saw the lights of the emergency vehicles surrounding the house. "I couldn't save him." She choked up at Arie, seeing Lilly over his shoulder with a look of concern.

He shh-ed her. "It's okay now. They know everything, okay? Everything will be all right."

And though she knew they were far from closing this case, she wasn't far.

Because as long as the Mastermind Murderer didn't exist in the world, there was no leader to the nightmares that had consumed her life.

And after today, Dill Jensen was finished.

She leaned into Arie and placed her head on his shoulder. She'd been here before, time and time again. At the end of what felt like the end. Only this time it was different. This time, as the blue and red flashing lights blurred in her line of vision, surrounded by the people who'd supported and loved her, she didn't feel as though she had more questions than answers.

For her, this was a new beginning.

EPILOGUE

1 Year Later...

The smell of her Mom's homemade stuffing wafted onto the front porch. Raine inhaled the savory rosemary combined with onion and peppers. Propped on the wooden porch swing, she pulled the knitted blanket tighter around her shoulders, and peered over the railing to the front lawn below.

Chloe leaped in the air on the lawn below the porch, catching a football and cradling it under her arm.

Raine laughed as her cousin bit the grass in an attempt to lunge for the flags that hung from Chloe's belt. Flag football was always a favorite holiday tradition for her family, and she sat in peaceful bliss that she was able to be home this Thanksgiving.

She couldn't get over how happy her sister looked. And though Chloe wore the bruises of the loss of Alex underneath her happy disposition and freshly colored lilac hair, she was still the same quirky, outspoken Chloe. It certainly helped that after Jensen was incarcerated and both his residences repossessed, they were able to gather enough evidence to convict Ray Olden, the bald-headed man, as the person who'd murdered Alex in the hit-and-run. Alex's death was finally brought to justice, rather than bearing the sinking feeling that he was brushed under the rug.

"Are you gonna daydream up there all day or what? C'mon! We're down a person!"

Raine shook her thoughts away and followed Arie's voice at the bottom of the stairs. "I'd rather just watch really, it's fine." She laughed, thinking how cute he looked with his "adopt, don't shop" sweatshirt on, and the flag football wings hanging at his waist. She had no doubts that he would fit right in with her family. And after more than a year of dating, she wanted nothing more than to have him here at the home she grew up in. It was a welcome break for both of them, before they had to head back to San Francisco.

After that day in the isolated desert, and after a much-needed break, Raine decided to leave her role as a clinical psychologist, and the practice she'd worked at with Marcus.

Marcus. Things were never the same between them. After the day she'd left him behind in the mansion, he kept his respectful distance from her. No evidence pointed to him ever working with the professor, so he wasn't considered part of the case, which Raine was glad to see. She viewed him as just another victim that had been manipulated in the game. She was happy that he went back to his practice and ran it with the integrity they'd always intended for it. He also respected her decision to resign.

And she had no regrets about moving on from the practice. It had been the absolute right choice. She and Arie had mapped out a business plan surrounding the animal shelter that he upkept. They were quite the team. He trained viable shelter dogs into therapy animals, and Raine would work with clients to introduce them to their new companions. For her, in this line of work, it was never a question whether she could help an individual. In this case, she was helping both the human and the animal find their mate, and their solace.

It was a field that was more fulfilling than she could have imagined.

After another whine in the background from her Dad, she threw the blanket off her shoulders and hopped off the porch swing. "All right! I'm coming. But you know I can't catch like Chloe, so don't get your hopes up!" The rush of the crisp, November air brushed her cheeks as she skipped down the stairs and retrieved the extra flags from Arie before joining the game.

She ran clear to the back of the field, hoping the ball never came that way. The view from up on the hill allowed her to see her whole family, playing and enjoying their tradition without a care in the world.

Throughout the years of nightmares she'd endured at the hand of one man, she'd only ever sought out closure.

That closure came in the form of a letter from a Lawyer, months after the case had closed. It stated that Dr. Dill Jensen had committed suicide while incarcerated, and that a large sum of money had been left in his will... to her. At first the thought disgusted her. She didn't want it. But after some thought, and a lot of legal juggling, she decided if there was going to be that large of an amount of money floating around somewhere, she better put it to good use. She decided to anonymously donate it to programs that aided in mental health.

There would be no plaque, no bench dedicated in the honor of Professor Jensen. And as time went on, nobody would remember his name.

As for Raine Walsh, she'd been able to close that chapter of her life and move on to a much brighter future. One that included homemade stuffing, surrounded by the ones she loved.

THE END

AUTHOR'S NOTE

Thank you for embarking on this journey with me. If you've made it this far, you've reached the end of The Mastermind Murderers series, for now.

As I sat in multiple psychology classes during my undergrad, the stories seemed to have written themselves, and characters appeared here and there in my head. I wanted to write a story with a non-typical hero; a strong female lead, who wore her flaws on her sleeve.

This series has been more than just a story for me, but a way to subconsciously express inclusion to a multitude of diverse characters in sexuality and race. I also intended to highlight social aspects that must change, specifically rape culture, among others.

Humans are connected to each other through life, death, and our emotional journeys. The human condition is our biggest flaw. But it is also our greatest gift.

Thank you for reading.

Until Next Time,
Kristin Helling

If you would like to hear more from Kristin Helling,
reach her here:
kristinhelling.com/subscribe

ABOUT THE AUTHOR

Kristin Helling enjoys stories with a journey- whether it's a journey across the globe, a journey through space, or a journey of finding one's self.

Kristin studied her Bachelors degree in English writing at Park University, and received an 18-hour minor in Psychology. Her favorite classes were *Positive Psych* and *Social Influence and Persuasion*. It was only a matter of time before this passion found its way into her fiction.

She is married to a photographer, and lives outside of Kansas City, Missouri with their two hairy children: a Husky who is terrified of vacuum cleaners, and a Collie-Shepherd mix with more energy than the sun.

www.ingramcontent.com/pod-product-compliance
Lightning Source LLC
Chambersburg PA
CBHW022158260626
47155CB00019B/3276

* 9 7 8 1 9 4 6 9 2 1 9 5 6 *